Crossing Roman

Genoa Mafia Series Book I

By Ginger Ring

Crossing Roman

Limitless Publishing, LLC
Kailua, HI 96734
www.limitlesspublishing.com

Formatting: Limitless Publishing

ISBN-13: 978-1-68058-889-7
ISBN-10: 1-68058-889-3

Dedication

To one of my favorite Mafia writers, Amy Rachiele.
Her suggestions for this book kept my bad boys bad
and the good parts even hotter.
Siete famiglia

Prologue

Madison

"What the hell was that?" Stephanie cried.

A blast from outside rattled several picture frames on the bridal shop wall.

Madison Miller rose and carefully removed the pins that lined her mouth from tacking up a gown's hem on the window mannequin. Her coworker's eyes were the size of saucers.

Footsteps trampled by the front door of the shop. Madison rushed to throw it open to see what the commotion was about. Fire roared, tearing up a car only a few shops away. The red flames licked the air around it, threatening everything in a three-foot radius.

"Holy crap." Stephanie, her best friend and assistant, was at her back craning to see.

A shopkeeper held a fire extinguisher and pointed it toward the blaze. Its small puffs of white barely touched the pyre that started off a typical retail day with a bang. A huge crowd started to encircle the inferno, keeping at a distance. Saturday shoppers got more than they bargained for today.

"Do you think anyone was in the car?" Stephanie hugged her arms across her chest.

"I don't know." Madison chewed her bottom lip.

"Did the gas tank explode?"

"I don't know," Madison snapped louder.

"It could spread." Stephanie continued watching the scene as she leaned heavily on Madison's back. She was right. The entire string of stores could be engulfed in flames, not leaving out the bridal shop Madison managed for her mother.

Thankfully, it was early and her typical influx of customers didn't show up until after lunch. She was just as intrigued and fearful as Stephanie and the rest of the bystanders. Within moments, sirens rang out and she exhaled. The town's warning siren blasted, calling all the volunteer firefighters in the area to service. Finally, after several minutes, help was on the way. A shiny red fire truck soon roared by and firemen began to fight the fire with a vengeance.

The buzz of the people on the sidewalk caught her attention. The horrific scene was difficult to tear away from, but her gaze darted into the onlookers and she froze. A tall, dark man in a finely tailored suit made her breath catch in her throat. She knew him. Seeing him again ignited a feeling that she wished to bury deep inside her—a combination of lust and alarm. It made her look away. Her heart pumped erratically at the quiet disruption of harmony in the little town of Genoa caused by both the fire and by this man. Comforted only with the authorities' arrival on the scene, Madison tugged on Stephanie's arm.

"Let's go in. The firetrucks are here. They will take care of it."

She dragged a reluctant Stephanie behind, but Madison stopped up short when her friend stood her ground.

"Hey, look." Stephanie pointed. Madison rolled her eyes. She'd seen enough and her anxiety level was at an all-time high. Biting her lower lip, she followed the direction Stephanie indicated only to freeze once again not at the sight of a man, but of a woman. Standing within the crowd, the young lady's profile made her go icy. The woman had shoulder length brown hair, light skin, and could basically be her sister. The lady even seemed to match her height from what she could tell from a distance.

"She could pass for your twin, Maddy." Stephanie still had her hand extended and Madison slapped her arm down.

"Come on. We have work to do."

"But."

"No buts. Let's go."

Madison shook everything off. The morning proved to be eventful and it was going to be a struggle to keep her mind on all of the dresses they had to great ready for upcoming weddings and fittings. It's just easier to shove it all down than deal with the bizarre goings on in town and in her life. Maybe later, at night, in the safety of her home, she'd think about it.

She stepped over the threshold of her shop with

Stephanie in tow. Even inside the warmth of the store, goosebumps rose on her arms. What was happening to her town?

Chapter One

January

One Month Earlier

When Madison got the call that they'd have to find a new place for bridal event, she wasted no time in driving over to discuss it face to face with the owner.

"What is the meaning of this?" She was on the verge of a breakdown. Her mother may have owned the only bridal store in the small town of Genoa, Wisconsin but that didn't mean their annual fashion show wasn't vital to attracting new customers. "I've booked your banquet center every year, year after year." She sat back in the chair and crossed her legs. "I paid the deposit months ago. What do you mean it's been cancelled?" Agitated, she swung her foot back and forth.

"Oh, I almost forgot." Mr. Gilmore, the club's owner, retrieved a check from his drawer and slid it across the desk. "Here's your money back."

"To hell with the money." Madison pushed the slip of paper back in his direction. "My spring wedding fashion show is always held here the second week of February." Her voice shook as the panic rose.

Find a new venue? Everything was set, from the DJ to the caterers. Heck, the ads were already in the paper. The cost alone to change them was going to hit her mother's pocketbook hard.

"We've had it here, for what?" She waved her hand in the air angrily. "Ten years in a row. How in the world can you say less than a month before the show the place is now booked? By who?"

"I'm sorry." The jerk thrust her deposit back in her direction and at least had the decency to look sheepish. "It can't be helped." His tone was firm.

This was a nightmare. It might be January, but it was still going to be a struggle to find a new place at this short of notice for her family business bridal show, the catalyst that drew new business every year. Not to mention her chance to show off some of her dress designs. It had been her lifelong dream to be a dress designer, but that dream was losing some of its sparkle. Her heart just wasn't in it as much as when she was younger and it was getting harder and harder to come up with new and exciting ideas.

She let her breath out loudly and shook her head. "You've put me in a horrible position. This show generates a massive portion of our revenue." Her voice shook with contempt at such a callous man. "All the new brides who got engaged over the holidays are looking for dresses and it's our chance to showcase our goods."

"I know." The dismissive idiot had the nerve to agree. "We've enjoyed hosting it all these years. I wish I could help out but my hands are tied." He folded his long fingers across his ample stomach.

His apology did zero to ease her misery. The asshole didn't realize how quickly this could spiral the bridal business she ran with her mother into the red. Nothing about this made sense. Madison snatched her check, shot to her feet, and rushed to the door.

She grasped the door handle to leave but made one final attempt to solve this wretched mess. "Do you know anyone, anyone at all who could host our event at this short notice?"

He leaned forward hesitantly and paused before saying, "Why yes. I do." The guy's smile spoke volumes. He was glad she was leaving.

"Firenza." Gilmore's response caused Madison to groan inwardly. "I believe it is available. The new place...you know, where the ball was held last year."

A flood of emotion tingled down her neck as she remembered the dance and the tall, dark, dangerous man who'd been there.

Mr. Gilmore leaned back in his chair. The wooden back screeched with his weight. "I was sure I saw you there. The company you kept was...interesting." What nerve. How dare he point out he saw her and insinuated about who she was with. "It would be a perfect spot."

"Thanks." She gritted her teeth. "I'll be sure to give them a call."

Madison mumbled to herself on the walk to her car. *Give them a call.* Never had she been so mad. If she were a gambling person, she'd bet it all that Roman Caponelli paid off Mr. Gilman to force her hand to reach out to his sister's venue, Firenza, for the bridal event.

Fastening her seat belt, she beat her fist against the steering wheel. Roman Caponelli, a man whose advances she'd rejected. *Mafia, my ass*. He'd just moved to town in the fall and was already trying to run the place.

She'd danced with him on the dreamlike night of the ball. Images of them gliding across the dance floor with his arms tucked around her made her lightheaded. The scent of his costly aftershave was forever locked in her brain. Just a whiff could make her knees weak.

But Madison did what she did best. She stuffed down the feelings he'd awoken in her because no matter how much electricity hummed between them when they were together, it didn't change the bottom line—that he was a front runner in the mafia.

She put the car in drive and hit the gas. Flying around the parking lot faster than she should, Madison came to the exit and slammed on the brakes. The heavy pile of snow on her roof slid down over her windshield.

"Damn," she muttered. "Can this day get any worse?" Her shoulders sank and she put the car in park. Huffing with annoyance, she got out of the car and flung the heavy snow off her car with the scraper. Usually she was careful about cleaning it all off the roof, but she'd been in a hurry knowing that her entire year's work was going down the toilet.

Settling back in her car seat, Madison backed up and parked her car. She didn't want to give up, and called a few of the other venues that were already programmed into her phone. Hope died more and more with each call. They were all booked. Of course they were all spoken for, because this was the type of luck she was having.

The last call was to Bells and Bows Wedding Shop, her mother's business.

"Stephanie, how's it going there?" Madison asked, hoping she'd have better news.

"I've got two wedding parties looking at dresses but other than that, things are under control. Did you get the venue straightened out?" Tittering women's voices could be heard in the din through the phone.

"No, we are S.O.L."

"What? The show is next month."

"I know." Madison sighed. "I'm at my wit's end."

"Did you try some of the others?"

"I called everyone I could think of and everything is booked. Maybe we can have it at the playground at McDonald's." Madison's breath frosted the tiny confines of her car and she stabbed the defrost button to clear her foggy windows.

"I hate to ask but...what about Firenza?" Stephanie knew the subject was a touchy one with her. She'd also been the first one to warn her of the Caponelli family reputation. Roman Caponelli, the man who'd swept her off her feet at the ball was the son of a mob boss and nicknamed Romeo for a reason.

Madison groaned out loud. "It looks like I don't have a choice."

"No, it doesn't. Sorry."

"Do you want to come with me?" The thought of seeing Roman again had her shaking in her knee-high boots.

"No. He knows how I feel about him so that probably isn't a good idea."

Madison's chin hit her chest. "Okay. I can do this. I can fix this." Madison wasn't actually sure whether she was reassuring herself or Stephanie.

"Good luck. Oh, and the cheese factory that's providing the hors d'oeuvres had a salmonella outbreak."

"What?" Madison widened her eyes. "Are you serious?"

"Afraid so." More laughter from the shop's customers sounded over the phone.

"I'll add that to my list." Madison groaned. "Well, I'd better go. I have to solve the first problem before I can think about the rest." A dull ache started to form in the back of her neck. Stress was building. No venue, no show, no money.

"Let me know what you find out."

"I will. Thanks, Steph. Bye." Tossing her cell in her purse, Madison drove her car to the one place she said she'd never go again, Firenza.

It wasn't that she hated the place; it was quite the opposite. Valentina, Roman's sister, had done a spectacular job renovating it. The new reception hall and summer restaurant was a remodeled old mansion with a very colorful past. It now had an updated Italian flare. The outside featured ivory stucco and a red tiled roof. During the warm weather, the grounds would be breathtaking with gardens, iron trim, and fountains.

After turning down Roman's advances on New Year's Eve, Madison hadn't talked to Valentina since. It had only been a few weeks, but she missed her new friend. They'd really hit it off fast.

Madison phoned the number of the restaurant at Firenza, but only the cleaning crew was there. A dead end. The venue issue needed to be solved or all the non-salmonella poisoned hors d'oeuvres would mean nothing without a place to put them. The Mr. Mouse Cheese Factory had a month to solve their issue which was doable. Finding a venue was next to impossible in such a short time. Chewing on her fingernails, Madison Googled more places that might be about to handle her event. Nothing. She even considered moving it completely out of the area, but her customers and clients would have to travel farther away and that could mean more loss of business.

She slammed her hand on the steering wheel again while emotions battled it out inside her head. Desperate, she had no choice but to go to the Caponelli homestead—or rather, *fortress*. The huge estate Roman purchased was set amongst the other mansions and villas along Lake Genoa. The small town of Genoa, Wisconsin, was a couple hours' drive from Chicago. A good portion of those living on the lake were wealthy inhabitants of the windy city that maintained beautiful homes on the enormous lake in the historic town.

The drive up to Roman's house, sans Tuscany castle, was halted by estate gates and a guard shack. Through the scrolled iron, Madison noted again, the three stories and sprawling compound. A six car garage sat around the back. She'd not seen the front, which faced the water up close, but she knew there was a boathouse to the side in the front with a large covered patio on top. Many times in the summer she'd taken boat rides with friends or walked the sidewalk that surrounded the entire lake.

"Welcome, Miss Miller." The man inside the tiny square guard house greeted her. He must have noted the stunned look on her face. She'd never met this man before but he knew who she was. He gazed down for a second before hitting the button that set the whir of a mechanism in motion and pushed open the large gates.

"Thank you." She waved cordially before pressing the gas pedal to propel the car forward up the winding brick driveway. Most of the homes were set way back from any main road. In the past, most people only lived at their lake homes in the summer and they were only accessible by water. Therefore their mail was delivered by boat. It was one of those old traditions that were still maintained and tourists even rode the mail boat as it cruised slowly around the lake. The quick footed delivery person would jump off the front of the boat, deposit the mail in the home owner's dock mailbox, and then jump into the back of the long boat before it sailed off.

One of Roman's bodyguards stood as a sentinel on the front steps as she pulled the car up to park. He opened her car door like he was a beefy valet with enough firepower under his coat to level a small building. Another man stepped forward and held a dog leash as it sniffed the wheels of her car.

"Hello, Arlo." Madison knew him. The man was a constant companion to Roman. Anytime she had been in Roman's company, Arlo was there. The guy was built like a freight train and practically reeked of testosterone. There didn't appear to be an ounce of fat on him, and he wore a permanent five o'clock shadow better than any male model.

Madison briefly considered taking her handbag, but instead left it in the car. The place smelled of money and no one here would be interested in the sixty dollars in her wallet or her dime store purse.

"Follow me." Arlo opened the door, and she was awed by the home.

Madison had only been there once before and that was after she'd been kidnapped. Andrea, an unlucky-in-love bride whom Madison once worked with, had been abused by her fiancé, Diego. After Madison convinced her to go to the police and call off the wedding, Diego went crazy, and kidnapped both Madison and his former bride-to-be. If it hadn't been for Roman and his men rescuing them, there was no telling what would have happened. She'd be forever grateful for them coming to her aid, but the image of Roman shooting Diego in the head with no remorse whatsoever would haunt her for a long time. The local police still suspected Roman in the monster's disappearance, but with no body and no one making a fuss about it, the case had been dismissed.

After they set her free, she fainted and found herself here, weak from lack of food and fear. Everyone had been kind to her, but there hadn't been time to take in the décor of anything other than the room she'd woken up in. Now she stopped and took in her surroundings. The place was open and airy. A few poinsettias dotted the tables while strands of holly still hung from doorways.

Like most people in the north land, Christmas decorations came down in stages. The tree was put away on New Year's Eve, but wreaths, plants, and greenery stayed around for as long as they lasted. One year Madison had forgotten to take down the wreath above her garage. After birds built a nest, it remained up until their babies flew away. Harming such fragile creatures appalled her even if it meant having a Christmas wreath up past Easter.

She wiped her snowy boots on a rug in the expansive foyer and trailed behind Arlo down a long hall. His broad shoulders made the hallway appear small even though it wasn't. Warm dark woods and burgundy accents carried out throughout the home's architecture. Expensive paintings dotted the wall between windows with breathtaking views of the lake. Madison barely missed bumping into Arlo's back when he stopped to knock on a door.

"Come in." The deep voice behind it sped up her heart. He was a dangerous man but at night she still dreamed of Roman's kisses. A flutter ripped through her lower belly thinking about what might have happened if she'd said yes to his pursuit. Arlo opened the door and motioned for her to enter.

Shaking off her nerves, Madison reminded herself why she was here. She marched into the room and planted her feet in front of his desk. He was just as gorgeous as the last time she saw him. Even more so if that was possible.

"My fashion show is scheduled for next month and now my venue has cancelled my booking. You wouldn't happen to have had anything to do with that, now would you?"

Roman rose from his chair. He came around the front and leaned against his desk. The cover model of a gentlemen's fashion magazine couldn't hold a candle to his luscious appearance—lavender dress shirt, patterned tie, and black pants. Did he not own a pair of jeans? It was a Saturday. Her weekend attire was leggings and a fleece zip-up. In summer it was shorts, tee, and flip-flops.

"So accusatory." He dragged out his response smugly. "It's nice to see you too, Madison." The way her name rolled off his tongue always made her swoon. "You look beautiful as always." He gave her a once over as she folded her arms across her chest. A raspy laugh rumbled from his throat and her cheeks flushed.

She stomped her foot and a chunk of missed snow slid on the carpet. The man had her flustered like a teenager with her first crush.

"Uh…thanks," she said, feeling less than beautiful and even more anxious. Madison shoved her hands in her pockets to keep from running and jumping in his arms. If she focused on their last knee-weakening kiss, she'd be a goner. Her mother's business was at stake. "Did you do that? It's been held there each year. My mother's business depends on that show."

He shrugged his shoulders with a confidence that couldn't be taught.

"If your venue is unavailable, you are welcome to use Firenza free of charge."

"How charitable of you." Folding her arms in front of her again, she paced the room.

"I am charitable."

"A man in organized crime." Madison used air quotes for emphasis. "Charitable. *Hmm*."

"Firenza is my sister's place. It's a legitimate establishment." His eyes narrowed and flashed with anger. "The family business does not affect hers."

"How much?" She had no choice but to take it, but it would not be for free. There was no way she wanted to be indebted to the family.

His lips spread wide in a panty dropping grin.

"Consider it a gift from my sister. Valentina would be more than happy to help you out of a bind."

She found it hard to believe anything from a crime family was free. There had to be a price to pay or a future favor to be asked.

"Really?" She narrowed her eyes and tilted her head to the side.

Roman pushed off from the edge of his desk and wandered way too close, invading her space. Sultry aftershave of an enticing mixture of musk and pine wafted to her nose. She inhaled deeply, letting it wash over her. Was it bad that she wanted to jump his bones? He was so wrong for her. He stood for everything she didn't, but there was something about the man that drew her in to the point he could make her sin and never regret a second.

What was it he'd said the first time they met in the coffee shop? She was debating over her favorite piece of cake and he whispered behind her, *"Sometimes doing what you want is worth the guilt."* Oh how she wanted to do things with him that would leave her feeling guilty and loving every minute of it.

"Why don't you have dinner with me and Valentina this evening? I'll cook." His smile made her knees weak. "We could discuss the logistics of your event."

He made a good case, but she wasn't fooled for a minute.

"As long as Valentina is here, I'll be here."

Chapter Two

Roman

"Cold out today," Arlo mumbled.

"Huh?" Roman tuned out the man driving. "What'd you say?" He still reeled from seeing Madison. He loved the boldness she displayed by showing up at his house. Trapping her to keep her there flickered through his mind. The woman crawled under his skin and stayed there. Her showing up today was a bonus to the otherwise boring events.

"The weather. It's cold out today." Arlo, his enforcer, kicked the heat up a little higher in their vehicle.

"It's January in Wisconsin. It's going to be cold. We should've left earlier. I'm never going to get all this shit done."

"What's on the list?" He started to tap the brake long before the intersection. The roads were still a little slick after last night's snow.

"We have to swing by Gessner's."

"The cheese maker?" Arlo eased onto the interstate and pressed the pedal to the floor, constantly checking the mirrors for followers. The vehicle was bulletproof but neither of them wanted to test it.

"Yeah. Too bad he fell on hard times and had to borrow. Alvin's making his final payment today." Roman started out like most guys in the business, breaking fingers and legs of those who couldn't pay. It was nice to know this man was able to keep up.

His cell rang. The image on the phone was that of his sister. "Valentina. What's up?"

"Roman." Her voice was hoarse.

"What's wrong?" It didn't sound like her.

"I'm in bed. I caught a bad cold. I hope it's not the flu." Her voice muffled into the phone as she coughed.

Roman groaned and scratched his forehead. "Did you send Uncle Matteo flowers yet?" Their favorite uncle was in the hospital.

"I haven't done anything." She sniffed into the phone. "I've barely been out of bed."

"Where are you?"

"I'm at Mom and Dad's." Their parents' home was in Chicago.

"Shit. I need you." He groaned and ran his fingers through his hair. "Dammit, I invited Madison over to discuss her bridal show. I told her you'd be there and she could use Firenza."

"Ha, you are never going to convince her to date you, Romeo." He hated that nickname. It meant he was a player. Maybe he fucking was, but he would

19

reconsider it if he could have another chance with Madison. She was the one who got away and the one he intended to catch. "You are playing with fire, getting her bridal show banned from every place in town." This time she coughed into the phone. "Shame on you."

"I have no shame and you agreed to help me." He exhaled and scowled out the window. The gray sky matched his mood perfectly.

"I'll help you with anything. You are my brother, but I never said this was a good idea." Another coughing fit started. "I've got to go." The phone went dead.

He beat his fist against the dash. "Son of a—" Then he rested his elbow on the arm rest. Roman was a man used to control, even if it was the location of a fucking bridal show. Madison needed to learn. Ever since he spotted her heart-shaped ass as she bent over, staring at the cake counter in the coffee shop, she'd been on his mind. From the first time he stared into her deep blue eyes, he was intrigued. Why, he wasn't sure. Maybe it was the fact that she was so far removed from the underworld he lived in. Maybe because she was a small town girl with a special innocence about her. Or maybe it was the fact that she was a challenge. She'd turned him down, but he wasn't taking no for an answer.

"Now what?" Arlo kept both hands on the wheel as they drove.

"Valentina's sick." Roman tapped a finger against his chin. "Firenza was supposed to be her thing, not mine."

His driver chuckled.

"What's so funny?"

"You. You got it bad for Madison and you won't stop until you get her."

It was all true, but what would happen after he had her? Would he want to move on to the next like he usually did? For some reason, he suspected the answer would be no.

Madison was someone who had her own life, her own business, and her own dreams and ambitions. She had choices Roman didn't. His life was already planned out. Hell, his father was putting pressure on him to get married and soon. His father wanted him to marry and unite his strong family to another one—the Rinaldis. The family needed an heir. Being the son of Don Caponelli had never been easy. The arranged marriage his father pushed for was something he couldn't comprehend. If he was getting married, it would be on his terms and to the one he wanted to spend his life with and no one else.

When Madison popped back in his mind, he smiled. She was beautiful—tall, curvy, with thick shoulder-length brown hair. Her skin reminded him of fine china. He'd never asked about her parents, but there was something about her that made him think she might have some Italian heritage somewhere in her background.

"What? You're not going to deny it?" Arlo joked and took the off-ramp to Milwaukee.

"No." Roman wasn't denying anything.

"Good. I like her." Roman lifted an eyebrow as he listened to his friend. "Girl's got spunk," Arlo added.

"Well, that's good you like her. I have to get her to like me." That had never been a problem before. He was used to getting any woman he wanted, anytime he wanted. At age thirty, he yearned like a bastard for a more meaningful relationship—a partner in life. The old school, traditional prearranged family bit the big one. His parents' marriage was arranged many years ago. Roman knew after only spending a short time with Madison that she may be the one. He couldn't explain it, he just knew it. She complemented him. The only problem was that sweet girls with ambition and goals didn't fall for bad boys whose lives were already planned. They wanted their own control. Frustration slammed into his chest. He couldn't change what he was, but he was determined to show her what kind of man he could be for her.

The hearty smell of cheese hit his nose as the bell jingled on top of the door of Gessner's.

"Roman," the man behind the counter yelled. "Welcome. It's good to see you." Alvin Gessner had been a friend of Roman's father for years. They'd gone to school together and both had followed each in their own family's business. The cheesemaker had been successful for years until the economy went bust and they lost some valuable restaurant and specialty food store accounts. The banks weren't loaning money and the family stepped in to provide the cash. Thankfully, Gessner had been able to keep up with the payments. It would have been hell if he couldn't. Roman didn't want to leave Alvin's wife a widow. He liked the family. Always had, but business was business.

Alvin's wife, Judy, was wrapping cheese. She looked in his direction and smiled. "Roman. Hello."

"Al, Judy, you're both looking well."

Alvin came around and shook hands with both men. "Wait here." The guy patted him on the shoulder and headed for the office.

"How have you been, Judy?" Roman tasted a piece of cheese off the sample tray. The Asiago here was the best. They even carried chocolate cheese made with cream cheese. Madison would love that. How easily she popped in his head, and seeing her today had his thoughts on overdrive.

Judy wiped her hands on her apron. "Busy. You know…with the holidays. So many cheese trays." She used both hands for emphasis.

"That's good." He tried the parmesan this time. The hard cheeses made him think of Madison again and the front of his pants tightened imagining her. If it weren't for his long coat covering himself, it would've been an awkward moment for sure.

"Here you go." Alvin came back in the room. He carried a thick envelope in one hand and a box in the other. He handed both to Arlo but addressed Roman.

"What's this?" Roman wondered about the box.

"I boxed up some of our specialties for you." The man was all smiles.

"Thanks, Al. Good doing business with you." He shook his hand again and nodded to his wife. It was a relief that the money was paid and their account now closed.

Roman and Arlo left. It was already dark out and

they had to haul ass to get home in time. They drove the rest of the way home in silence. Roman's heart rate ticked at an exhilarating rate. He was going to see Madison at seven. He had to prepare. Everything had to be perfect for his spit-fire.

"You need to pick up Madison at six-thirty," Roman ordered Arlo as a reminder.

"Yeah, I'll be there."

Roman tapped his finger on the dash. He was on edge. It was like how he felt before a hit, only this time the target was the woman he hoped would fall in love with him.

Chapter Three

Madison

The knock on the door nearly made her jump out of her skin, as if she wasn't nervous enough. Madison was equally pissed and excited at the same time. At least Valentina would be there. She'd been concentrating so hard on her makeup that the knock scared her half to death. Her hair brush hit the floor and she cursed. It was pure luck that she was already done lining her eyes or there would have been a black mark halfway across her face, or worse yet, she'd be missing an eyeball. Giving one last look into the full-length mirror, she grabbed her purse and hurried down the stairs.

By the time she'd reached the main floor, her guest had switched to the doorbell.

"Coming." Madison slid across the linoleum floor in her tights, her leather boots in one hand. Flinging open the door, she came face to face with a frowning Arlo.

"Hello." She'd hoped Roman would be the one

standing before her, but she kept the disappointment out of her voice. "Arlo." Obviously he didn't care enough to pick her up himself. One boot slipped through her fingers and landed with a loud thump.

"Something came up that Romeo had to handle himself."

Madison shrugged off the Romeo reference and motioned for Arlo to come in. She sat on the vintage ottoman by the coffee table to slip on her knee-high boots.

Displeasure was all over his face as he stepped in and closed the door behind him.

"Is something wrong?" she clipped, annoyed Roman didn't have the decency to pick her up himself. She zipped up one boot and now struggled with the other.

"You should never open the door without first checking to see who it is." He scolded her like she was a twelve-year-old.

"It's a small town." She dismissed his advice with a zip of the last boot. "Hardly anything ever happens here."

"Is that so?" The guy was so big he filled the entire doorway. "Wasn't it just a short time ago that we had to save you from the bastard who kidnapped you. He would have killed you." Arlo's voice rose uncharacteristically.

She'd tried to forget that horrible experience. But it did little to simmer her anger.

"I'm fine. Thank you for your brutish words of wisdom."

"There's nothing brutish about it. As Romeo's woman, you will be a target and you can't ever forget it." He pointed a thick finger at her for emphasis.

Madison rose to attention. "What did you just say?" Her voice was low and menacing, shocking herself as well as Arlo. His woman? "Thank you for the advice," she added with sarcasm. Her teeth clenched. "But I am *not* Roman's woman." Arlo could refer to him as Romeo, but she never would.

Arlo laughed and held her coat for her. "What Roman wants, Roman gets."

"Well, what Madison wants, Madison gets and what Madison wants is a venue for her show." Her words were venomous. "And that's the only reason I am dining with the devil." She really didn't consider Roman the devil, but right now she was pissed.

Arlo just smiled, ignoring everything she said.

"Besides Valentina, their mother is great at event planning." He guided her out the door and toward the car.

"Really." Her words held no true interest until it struck her. She never thought of Roman as having a mother. He was larger than life at times, feared, respected. It was hard to imagine him as a toddler dragging a teddy bear around and referring to someone as *Mom*. It was more like he'd been plopped down on the earth by some monster temptress intent on causing turmoil and chaos on her emotions.

"So both of his parents are alive?"

"Yes, very much so." He waited until she buckled her seat belt before closing the car door. "I'm sure you will meet them soon enough," he added when he got in and started the engine.

"I doubt it." The vehicle rocketed out onto the vacant street.

"I don't," he quipped back.

She rolled her eyes. The man seemed too sure of that fact.

It was just a short drive to Roman's and they were there before she knew it.

"I've been with Roman since we were kids. You're the first woman he's ever cooked for."

Arlo waved to the guard in the shack and the estate gates groaned as they opened. He raised a congenial hand to the man who patrolled the front entrance of the estate. "Us guys, yeah, but never for a woman," he continued. "Well, besides Valentina. Never," he stressed again as he pulled up front and put the car in park. "I guess that makes you special or something."

'Or something' is right. She pondered that one, but not for long, as Arlo had already come around and opened her door. Madison shaded her forehead against the glare of the outside lights. "Wow, they're bright."

"We like to see when people are coming." He motioned to the neighboring homes. "Notice the difference. Our lights are brighter, the shrubs shorter, and nothing to hide behind close to the house. We also have motion detectors, dogs, and lots of cameras."

"What are you all so scared of?" She frowned.

"Absolutely nothing." He chuckled.

Not bothering to knock, Arlo rang the doorbell and then waved at an overhead camera. The door immediately unlocked and she was ushered in.

"Relax. We also have bulletproof doors and windows. Nothing can get you from outside these walls."

It wasn't what was outside the walls that she was concerned about. Roman's deep voice rumbled in the distance.

"Follow me." Arlo took her coat and led the way. Roman's home appeared even larger at night.

"You need to supply maps to the guests or a GPS." Madison's flippant words didn't appear to bother Arlo. She'd only seen part of the house this morning. Each visit gave her bits and pieces of how really big it was.

The same warm tones that were in the other areas, she'd seen continued throughout. A mammoth-sized dining table filled one room. She could almost hear the laughter and clicking of silverware that would go on in a place this big during Thanksgiving or Easter dinners.

"Is Valentina here yet?" Her nerves kicked into gear. Having another female around would help her to calm down and ease the chip off her shoulder for having to stoop to dinner with the mafia prince.

"No. She's not coming."

"What?" She halted. "Did Roman put you up to this?" Madison jabbed a finger at the enormous man's chest. Roman had no morals. Why would she think he wouldn't say anything to get what he wanted? What a fool she'd been.

"No, she's ill. She probably needs a doctor."

Madison apologized and placed her hand over her heart.

"I hope it isn't anything serious?" Despite the family tree, she really was fond of Valentina.

"Like everyone in the family, the girl is an overachiever. She's been studying for the Bar exam." Madison shook her head and gasped.

"Bar? As in law school?" She really felt out of place being around this family of killers and overachieving lawyers. Valentina was going to be a lawyer and had an event center to run. Madison still ran her mother's small town bridal shop while its owner spent most of the year down south or wherever her latest whim had taken her. She'd never resented her mother's extravagant lifestyle until now. Madison was thirty and what did she have to show for it? Nothing.

"Yes, she's always loved school."

"That is definitely ambitious. How's she going to be a lawyer and run Firenza at the same time?"

"She'll only have one client."

They'd stopped in the dining room as Roman's conversation, in Italian, resonated in the background. Arlo obviously didn't want to disturb him yet.

"One client? That hardly seems worth it to go through all that work for only one client." Madison knew the answer to the question before she'd finished asking it.

"She will be legal counsel for the Caponelli family." Arlo confirmed her suspicions. It made perfect sense, in fact, to a fault. With the various legal and illegal parts to their businesses, they would want someone they trusted to handle the details.

From the expression on Arlo's face, it appeared that it was now safe to enter the kitchen. "You may go in and make yourself comfortable. He shouldn't be much longer." With a slight nod of his head, he added, "Enjoy your evening."

On shaky legs, she entered the home's well-lit kitchen. Roman stood with his back to her, his attention on the call and the view outside the window. There were bright lights in the front yard as well. It was hard not to be affected by his presence, and she hated herself for it. He was so bad for her, yet he was impossible to resist. His words in Italian almost sounded like erotic poetry. If he whispered sweet nothings in her ear in that language, there was a good chance she'd melt like an ice cream sundae in August. Madison knew she would have to be careful. He was too tempting.

She admired Roman's long legs in the jeans he wore. How could something so commonplace be so extravagantly appealing? Apparently, he did own something other than finely tailored suits. Of course, the jeans fit to perfection as well. She licked her lips. Uncomfortably warm, Madison forced her gaze to travel upward from his firm behind to his wide shoulders. An ivory sweater that stretched with the strain of his muscles completed his outfit. It looked soft and cozy. The kind of thing a girl would want to rest her head on as she watched a late night movie and ate popcorn.

Madison frowned. It was no use trying to deny that the man fascinated her. He was the proverbial flame to her moth. His nearness threatened to burn her if she got too close. Already her cheeks were hot and her focus again fell to his firm butt. A moan escaped her lips. Heat flushed her chest and he turned to face her. He'd caught her staring. Roman grinned and winked when he locked eyes with hers. She failed to notice he was no longer on the phone.

"Welcome." Roman approached, his arms open. Madison stiffened for a hug but instead he leaned in, placed his hands on her upper arms, and dropped a gentle kiss to both her cheeks, sending a tingle that made goosebumps rise on her skin.

"Hello." Madison forced herself to loosen up. She stepped back, not wanting the heat of his body so close.

"Dinner will be ready soon." Roman's eyes captured hers. In the depths of them, he seemed a mischievous little boy and happy to have her there.

"Thank you." Madison didn't know what else to say now that she was here in his kitchen. Naturally, it was just as impressive as the rest of the house. Everything was shiny and clean which made it appear to have been recently remodeled from ceiling to floor. Intricate tiles gave it a Mediterranean feel. Again there were flashes of burgundy and dark woods here and there. Madison took the liberty to stride around the huge space.

Plants sat near the window. No, make that small spice filled crocks. It must be wonderful to be able to walk over and snip off a sprig of basil or parsley whenever one needed it. Madison had never been much of a cook, but having all the tools of the trade nearby was definitely appealing. Except for the commercial size stove, no stainless steel appliances were in sight. Every piece of domestic equipment was framed with matching woodwork.

A large pot bubbled and hissed on a wrought iron grate atop the stove.

"Smells delicious." Madison walked over to peek inside. It appeared to be spaghetti and the large faucet over the stove had probably been recently used to fill it. One of those would be nice in her home. Of course, cooking pasta for one would probably not make it worthwhile.

"Bolognese," Roman announced, coming closer to Madison.

The meaty tomato mixture filled her senses with the tangy aroma of basil, oregano, and peppers. Her mouth watered and her stomach groaned. The slight sting of garlic tickled her eyes as she hovered over the pots. Hints of fresh baked garlic bread lingered in the air too.

It was easy to picture herself in Italy as some Italian opera played in the background. The kitchen's décor, the ethnic foods, and the chef speaking in his native tongue all came together for an amazing break from the stress of the day. Madison leaned against the corner and returned her attention to Roman. She'd had no idea what he was talking about on the phone, but it sounded just as delicious as the meal simmering on the stove. It was amazing that he spoke so fluently, yet had no accent of any kind.

He glanced her way and smiled. "I'm glad you came."

She'd been caught admiring him again. The whole situation was awkward. Madison grabbed a spoon to stir the sauce. Whether or not it needed it, she had to keep her quivering hands busy and it felt like she was helping. Soon the fragrance of the food was blended with a piney whiff from his cologne. Roman was close, too close. He stood behind her. It was too intimate and bordered on romantic. Madison slipped out from in front of him.

"Can I help you with anything?" she asked, her voice pitched high and awkward.

This situation was more difficult than she could have imagined. Roman was too tempting, too attractive and she was standing in his kitchen feeling like a nervous sheep in front of a large wolf.

"Just keep stirring the sauce." Covering her hand in his, he skimmed the foam off the top of the simmering tomato sauce and poured it into a nearby bowl.

"Why are you doing that?" She stared at both of their hands bonded together, the tingles making her lightheaded.

"It gets rid of the acid in the sauce."

"Oh, I think I can handle this. You probably have something else to tend to."

He chuckled and finally released her hand.

"I will slice the bread then." Roman didn't move away, though. Instead, he lightly pushed her hair from in front of her shoulder to the back. Taking her gaze off the bubbling pot, she glanced up into his eyes. His stare wasn't deadly like his reputation. It was intense, passionate, and intoxicating.

A timer sounded. Madison jumped and clutched her hands to her chest.

"The bread is done." His lip curled into a breathtaking smile.

Roman used a padded mitt to remove a crusty loaf of garlic bread from the oven. Madison lightly touched her lips—an act both involuntary and wistful.

"I think we are ready to eat." He steered her out of the kitchen and into a screened in porch overlooking the lake. Candlelight flickered from various sconces and candleholders scattered around the room. Bright lights out front spotlighted the lingering snow, while moonlight glistened off the ice of the lake. It must have been an amazing vista to sit here in the morning sipping coffee. The romantic feel of the room overwhelmed her and her breathing increased. The urge to flee was strong but she couldn't move if she wanted to. She was in way over her head with this man. How easy it would be to fall for this dangerous guy. His kind efforts made it harder and harder to stay angry with him.

Madison had agreed to dinner but she hadn't agreed to more, especially not with him. She had to be strong. For so long she'd arranged other couples' weddings, but planning hers had crossed her mind more than she cared to admit since meeting Roman. He wasn't the type of family man she had hoped for. Despite this, he was charming, smart, and charismatic.

"Is something wrong?" He poured red wine into her glass.

"No." She took a big sip of liquid courage, while examining him over the rim of her glass.

Roman laughed and refilled her glass to the top when she set it down. "Are you sure? You didn't even wait for the toast."

"A toast?" Madison didn't like the sound of that. "For what?"

"*Salud*. To new beginnings." Roman tapped his glass against Madison's. The pricey crystal pinged like a fine wind chime.

"I'm not sure what you mean." Immediately, her thoughts raced to analyzing things he had said.

"Valentina's Firenza. Your new venue for your bridal event, of course."

"Oh.…Thank you." Was she the only one who was having a problem concentrating?

"Let's eat." Roman motioned toward the table and wandered over to pull a chair out for her.

After she was seated, he left and quickly returned with the fresh bread cut and spread on a platter. A twirl of steam rose from the center. The shiny plates reflected the light from the candles. A small dish of olive oil with grated cheese accompanied the hot slices.

"Here, try some while I get the rest." He placed a generous piece on her plate.

"Do you need any help?" It was odd for her to be waited on. The urge to jump up and help was automatic.

"No, just eat," Roman called from the other room. She gave in to temptation. The bread crushed with the first bite and flaky pieces tickled her tongue. It was just the way she liked it—crispy on the outside and soft on the inside. Her taste buds sang Italy's national anthem and a moan of culinary pleasure hummed from her lips.

Madison was tearing apart the second piece with her fingers by the time Roman returned with two plates. Her eyes widened at the size of the portion on her plate. The meat-filled red sauce covered a generous amount of pasta. "I'm not sure I can eat all this."

He raised his wine glass. "*Mangia*." Roman settled into his seat and she touched her goblet to his. The click of glass again echoed in the room. "You had a long day. Enjoy."

"How would you know?" Her spine stiffened.

"You were obviously upset when I saw you last." His compassion unnerved her just as much as his strength.

"I had good reason to be. The man gave away my venue. Speaking of which, we are supposed to be talking about my event." Madison took a sip of wine. "Valentina was supposed to be here."

"Would you have come if it were any other reason than business?"

"No." She'd said it, but did she really mean it?

Roman sat back in his chair. He wore a hurt expression briefly before it vanished as quickly as it had appeared.

"Then I'm glad you had no choice but to use Firenza."

The man was infuriating. Even with such an appealing dish in front of her, she suddenly couldn't eat a bite.

Roman placed his fork on the table. "What's wrong?"

"This." She waved her hand in the air. "I shouldn't have come." Madison stood and Roman did also.

"I thought you were hungry?"

"I am and this looks delicious but I can't do this." She tossed her napkin on the table.

"Do what?"

"Valentina is not here. This was a business meeting. It was a mistake to come here. Please have her call me when she's feeling better." Madison strode toward the kitchen.

"Have dinner with me. Don't let all this good food go to waste." She heard a twinge in his voice. The man didn't give up. Madison stopped short.

Her lips trembled. "I know how you work, Romeo Caponelli. You wine and dine women, they fall for you, and then you leave them by the curb with the trash."

"Don't call me that," he scolded, and she knew she'd crossed a line. "Romeo was a weak man. He didn't even have the decency to die a respectable death. Poison." He swore. "His woman was braver than he with a dagger to the chest." He slammed his fist against his sternum. "I don't want that. Not from you." He lowered his head and sighed. "Yes, in the past…that was Romeo, the boy. I'm now Roman, the man."

"Well, I don't need a man with a past." Madison definitely didn't need that.

"What do you want Madison?"

She wanted him, but she didn't need what came with him.

"What I need is a man who is content with living and raising a family in a small town. Genoa is a safe place where people know their neighbors, but some people might think it is boring."

"I don't think anything like that about you, and I

don't think this town is boring. I am at the point in my life where I do want to settle down and raise a family. Genoa seems like a perfect place."

"But the mafia and your past…" She wasn't letting it go.

The tension in the air was thick enough to slice with the serrated bread knife he'd just used.

A few seconds hung in the air before he spoke. He calmed. "I'm sorry. Please sit down." He gestured to the chair she'd vacated but Madison stood her ground.

"Okay, I can't change who my family is and I've had girlfriends. Just as there have been men in your life, I'm sure. Don't let the past hurt the future. Please, have dinner with me. It's all that I ask."

She nodded, her eyes brimming with tears. Why was she so emotional? This wasn't like her. Madison swung around and did as he asked. Roman settled into his chair and picked up a fork.

"I had no idea that Valentina was sick. I apologize if you feel that you were deceived. It was not my intention." Roman didn't strike Madison as a man who apologized too often. "Maybe I should have suggested we do this another night, but I'm being sincere when I say I wanted to see you."

Madison sat speechless, her mind still not made up.

"Please eat." He waved his hand across the table. "I cooked this especially for you."

She still didn't move.

"Have you eaten anything today?" he asked.

Madison shook her head. Her chin fell to meet her chest.

"Eat." It wasn't a request.

She sniffled, angry with the threatening tears. This was so not her. Was it the man or her hormones that had her all out of sorts?

He took a sip of wine. "To me, control is everything," he started. Madison's face lifted at the turn of the conversation. She hated being in control all the time. How easy it would be to have someone else shoulder some of the reasonability.

"When you were kidnapped, I'd never felt so useless and vulnerable. The thought of something happening to you…" He shook his head and bit into a piece of bread. Why was he bringing that up? Madison battled with that nightmare every single day. In just a few hours, it had been mentioned twice—by Arlo and Roman.

"Don't ever let your guard down again," he warned, and then softened. "Promise me." His eyes glared into hers.

"I promise." Her lower lip trembled and she picked up her fork. Madison and Roman ate in silence. The only sounds in the room was of utensils clicking on the plates. The quiet was deafeningly loud.

She couldn't take it any longer and finally spoke. "So why did you really come to Genoa? It had to be more than just opening a restaurant."

"My father is getting older. Soon I will be taking over the business. I want to move the family into a more legitimate business."

"That's good to hear." If only that were true. "So what are you thinking?"

Roman spoke up and had several good ideas, all

of which made sense to her. Restaurants, jewelry stores, car dealerships. Although the bridal business had never been her choice to go into, she did excel at it. The chance to brainstorm for options to move his family toward more respectable areas was invigoration to say the least.

"What do you think I should do?" The question took her off balance. He was the one who demanded control, yet he was asking for her advice.

She bit her lip and thought for a moment. "Wineries. The state is becoming a big force in the wine industry." Who didn't enjoy wine?

"That's a great idea. I will look into that." Roman's mouth was firm.

His quick acceptance of her suggestion caused her to puff her chest out and his gaze dropped briefly to her breasts. He took a drink of wine and seemed to study her over the glass.

"Was your dad Italian?" Roman asked out of the blue.

She shrugged her shoulder. "I don't know. Why?"

"You just have a look about you, like there's an olive tree in your ancestry."

"I wouldn't know. He died before I was born and my mother refuses to tell me anything about him."

"What was his name?"

She plopped a piece of fresh mozzarella from the dish on the table into her mouth and closed her eyes in culinary pleasure. Madison loved cheese.

"You're going to laugh," she said.

"Why?" He rested his elbow on the arm of his chair, seemingly curious about what she had to say.

"It's Smith. John Smith." Her face reddened and her eyes lowered. "I know, it's the most common name in the world." It sounded lame even to her. It stung when she thought about the times she'd asked her mother for more information. Was her father some man her mother met, a one-night stand, or had he really died in an accident? It always nagged at Madison, but she couldn't just fault her mother. No one had stopped Madison from doing her own search for the man. It was just easier to not know.

Chapter Four

Roman

John Smith, my ass. Roman couldn't stop the smirk that lifted the corner of his mouth, and he quickly lowered it before she could notice. Not knowing Madison's mother, it was hard to tell if that was the truth or not but something didn't seem right.

"So Miller is your mother's last name?" It obviously wasn't Smith.

"Yes," she replied.

Her skin glowed under the gentle flicker of the candlelight. He'd tried to stay away. She was so different than anyone he'd ever pursued and maybe that was what lured him to her. No woman ever turned him down, and the vulnerable side of Madison drove him mad. He wanted her but it was more than that. He wanted to protect her, take care of her, and love her. Roman did everything he could to not think of her again. She deserved better than him. Madison needed peace and stability. One of those guys who left at night to hang with the guys, not because he had "business" to tend to or someone to kill.

Try as he may, he couldn't stay away. She calmed him and intrigued him like no other. Since the first time he laid eyes on her, life had been torture.

The thought of someone else coming into her life sent his temper into a frenzy. Fighting it had become too much. He'd done the only thing he could think of; he made her come to him. It was devious and childish. However, it worked. He cursed himself for being a coward, but manipulation was a specialty of his. Making others do what he wanted was a game he'd learned at an early age. Now he felt like a heel for forcing her to have her show at Valentina's club. He'd never considered how much stress it could put on her. With a bit of luck, he'd be able to make it up to her somehow and the meal was his first attempt.

"I hope you left room for dessert." Roman slid back his chair and headed for the other room.

She groaned. "I don't think I can eat another bite."

Madison may have said she was full, but that didn't stop her from picking her fork up after he placed a piece of chocolate cake in front of her. "You made this?" Her eyebrow lifted.

"I'm afraid I can't take credit for this one. It's from the coffee shop." The first time he'd ever laid eyes on that luscious backside of hers, she'd been debating over a sinful looking chocolate layer cake at the Genoa Java Shop all those months ago. This was the same kind of cake.

"You remembered." Her voice held surprise and appreciation.

Her smile made his efforts worthwhile. He only needed to think of a way to manipulate his way into a second date.

"After all this food, I'll have to take two trips around the lake."

"I think you look perfect just the way you are."

"That's because I'm covered in layers of sweaters." She swiped her hand down the front of her but the comment didn't deter her finishing the cake.

"Do you walk around the lake often?" It was a good twenty miles around, so people tended to just do short sections at a time. Even though the area in which he lived was far from the heavily traveled areas, it was the path that Madison usually took. He'd be lying if he said he didn't take his morning coffee by the window hoping he might see her shapely, yet slender figure walking or jogging by early in the day. If he did spot her, it was the highlight of his week.

"I try to walk every day to clear my head and I run several times a week. When it's not too cold, of course."

"Of course." Roman kept his gaze locked on her face, enjoying her savoring the cake. She did everything with such passion. He quickly shut down the thought about what other things she might do with such fervor.

"What about you?" Her brown eyes were even darker in the candlelight.

"I exercise here. Boxing, weight lifting, and martial arts."

Madison slowed her chewing and put her fork down.

"Do those estate gates and walls keep people out?"

"That's the reason most people have them for," he teased.

She leaned closer and rested her elbow on the edge of the table. "What about the path out front? What's to stop someone coming across the lawn?"

"Are you worried about me?" Hope sprang.

Slumping back in the chair, Madison folded her arms across her chest and shrugged. Maybe she did care.

"Don't be. We know when to be extra careful," he said, trying to calm her fears.

"But what about out there?" This time she pointed out the window.

"Cameras. Also motion sensors going both across the property from side to side and on the lawn. Small animals can sometimes set them off." He'd finished his dessert and pushed the plate away. "Unfortunately, if it is snowing, raining, or the lawn care company is here we have to turn them off." Roman leaned forward, locking eyes with her. "So does this mean that you at least care?"

"I never said I didn't." She sat back up.

"There are no guarantees in life, Madison. Anyone's home can be broken into. The security measures taken here are necessary." He waved his hand. "You are safer in my home than in yours. I know you don't know what to think about me and my family, but if you ever need anything, anything at all, always know that you can come to me for help."

Her gaze lowered and she shook her head. It was a start. He reached out to grasp her hand with his. She turned to look out the window. "Let's go into the living room. How about watching a movie?"

"It's getting late." Madison wiggled in her seat. "I should go." This business dinner had spun into something that was way too personal. He felt it and she obviously did too.

Despite her disagreement, Roman led her by the hand into the living room. A crackling fire burned in the fireplace.

"I think that I should go." Flipping the television on, he passed her the remote, ignoring her request to leave. "Pick something."

The phone in Roman's pocket vibrated. He checked the screen. It was Arlo. Ignoring it, he sent a text saying he was not to be disturbed. After turning it off, he tossed it on the counter.

"I'll be right back."

"I really think—"

"Pick a show or movie and I'll be right back." It didn't take long to put the leftovers in the fridge and the dishes in the dishwasher. He had staff that would do the rest in the morning. These simple tasks gave him a sweet sense of home. When you do something mundane for someone you care about, it gives a sense of satisfaction that is unlike anything in the world. Roman loved his house, but without a wife and children it was just that, a house. He wanted a home.

The bread he held slipped from his hand. Wife? He'd had thoughts of it before but now that Madison was in his home, it made it more real. The arranged marriage shit wasn't going to happen. He wouldn't let it. He would make his father understand. Madison was an outsider, but he'd make it work. She would be able to fit in with the rest of the family and be accepted by them. The bottle of wine beckoned and he didn't bother to find a glass. The dessert wine was too sweet for his taste, but he swigged it anyway. If there'd been a brandy nearby, that would have been his first choice. Roman had a challenge in front of him. He knew what he wanted. He just needed to convince two other people—his father and Madison.

Roman turned off the lights. The combination of wine and spending more time with Madison had his blood pumping. In the living room, he scanned the area and stopped, his heart thumping. What the hell? He called her name and searched everywhere downstairs.

Cursing in two languages, Roman puffed out his cheeks and stormed back to the island in the kitchen. He grabbed his phone off the counter and punched in Arlo's name.

Arlo picked up on the first ring.

"What the hell happened?" Roman paced the room and headed for his office. "Where is she?" he yelled at the top of his lungs and punched his black walnut desktop.

"I'm taking her home." Arlo's voice was low.

"What the fuck? I didn't tell you to take her anywhere."

He was whispering. "No, but she did. I was outside the front door. Madison came out and asked me to drive her home."

Roman paced the room, stopped, and pinched his thumb and index finger on the bridge of his nose. The urge to order her back here was overwhelming, but she'd have no part of that. It would just piss her off. He'd have to be patient.

"I thought you knew." Arlo was apologetic.

"No. I didn't." He hated being patient. "Get your ass back here as soon as possible." He didn't bother to wait for an answer and tossed the phone across the room. The next time Madison stepped foot in his house, she'd be spending the night in his bed.

Chapter Five

Madison

Her town was her sanctuary, but today, she couldn't get away fast enough. As soon as the sun popped up, she was dressed and out the door. The need to flee was overwhelming. She had agreed to dinner but just being in the same zip code as Roman was too close. Damn it, their dinner had been too intimate. She'd had to leave. As much as her head refused to give in, her heart and body ached for his touch. She had to be strong. He was all wrong for her.

Madison rested her head on the car seat. As much as she tried to fight it, the one place she wanted to be was in his arms, but she'd done the right thing.

Raising her head, she ran her fingers through her messy hair. She'd left in such a hurry she hadn't bothered to even comb it. What did it matter?

Who cares what people think?

Stephanie knew Roman was Mafioso and made

her opinions on the matter very clear. Madison concentrated on the fact that Valentina owned Firenza and that's who she needed to work with, not her sexy brother. The man made her weak in the knees and her mother's absence made the whole situation with the show fall on her shoulders.

Madison backed her car out of the garage and headed north. The destination didn't matter. She just needed to go somewhere, do something. Putting miles between her and the man who never left her mind, gave her a chance to think. As she left town, the calm countryside numbed the tension flowing through her veins.

An hour later, Madison headed back to Genoa after clearing her head. A billboard for Valentine's Day caught her attention and she rolled her eyes. She had a love-hate relationship with Cupid's holiday. It was great for the business, as many people got engaged or married on February fourteenth. The loneliness of being single on that particular day of the year was like a knife to the heart.

She would never settle for someone who didn't make her heart sing when she heard their voice, and being with someone just so she had a companion in life was also not an option. Madison wanted more, and that more came with passion and love. Maybe she'd been too fussy all these years. Even if she lived the rest of her life alone, it was better to be by herself than to be with the wrong person. She wasn't going to settle for less than a soul mate. When the word soul mate came to mind, only one person's face came into view. Roman's.

Was she just like her mother? Connie never married. She never dated either. Her suspicious behavior never made sense. In essence, her mother was a stranger in many ways. She laughed out loud, thinking that maybe her mother was visiting a man all these years. They'd never been close but it wasn't too late to mend any bonds that had unraveled over the years. The calming effects of having taken a drive had dissipated as even more confusing thoughts bounced around in her head.

Her fist hit the steering wheel and the horn accidentally beeped. The cows in a nearby field raised their heads before returning to chewing the hay at their feet. She said a mental apology for disturbing their mid-morning meal, but she'd had more than she could take. Her foot hit the brake and she pulled her car to the side of the road, confused and dejected.

Roman had swept her off her feet the first time they met months ago and all while failing to mention he was from an organized crime family. The declaration betrayed her trust, but would it have made a difference?

Choosing not to be with him was torture. Her head said she didn't want to be with him but her heart said otherwise. It still irked her that he was trying to manipulate her back into his arms. The manipulation stung. Madison was her own woman and she planned to keep it that way.

She dug in her purse and pulled her cell phone out. To hell with Roman. Flicking through the list of contacts, she called Valentina.

It rang and rang. Madison's finger hovered over

the disconnect button, but Valentina finally picked it up.

"Hello." Her voice was raspy and low.

"Valentina?" Damn, she'd forgotten Valentina was sick. "I'm so sorry to bother you. I can call you another time when you're feeling up to it."

"No, that's all right." She cleared her voice before adding, "I'm just tired. I think the worst has passed."

"I'm glad to hear that. I missed seeing you last night."

"You too. I heard my brother cooked."

"It was delicious, but then you probably already know that."

"Not really. He has me do the cooking. I think he likes you," she teased. Did he really like her? *Business*, Madison chanted in her head. *Let's keep the conversation about business.* That was not what she needed to hear now and not why she called.

Silence stretched over the phone before Madison spoke up.

"I think he was just trying to make amends for the con he pulled on me." It sounded weak even to her.

"What con? Don't sell my brother short. When he wants something, he won't let anyone stand in his way and I'm pretty sure he has his sights set on you."

Madison shook her head and tried to focus. "I called to talk about the fashion show."

"Roman told me. I'm sorry. Bad luck for them and good luck for us." Excitement rang in her croaky voice. "It's going to be amazing."

53

"I think it was more than bad luck," Madison muttered. There was no need to place blame or complain. The fact remained. She had a venue and a beautiful one at that.

"What?" Valentina had a coughing fit. "I guess I'm still not over this thing yet."

"When you are feeling better, can we meet to go over the particulars? I'm anxious to make sure everything is in order."

"Didn't you discuss it with Romeo last night?"

"Umm. Not really. I felt you were the one to have the conversation with."

"Is it okay if I call you in a few days? Your event is booked and on the calendar, so don't worry about that." A whoosh of relief went through Madison.

"Call me when you're feeling better and we can plan. I will call and change the location with the caterers and florist."

"Great. I am glad your bridal event will be at Firenza. I love those types of affairs and I hope we will be hosting it every year."

"Thank you. See you soon."

Relief washed over Madison. It was done. The venue was set and she knew that Valentina wouldn't let her down. She was a professional when it came to Firenza.

She ended the call and stuffed her cell in her purse. A loud moo sounded outside her window and Madison noticed she'd acquired a crowd. Outside her car, a line of curious Holsteins had wandered over to see what all the fuss was about. With a quick wave to the bovines, she put her car in drive and returned to the road. She was heading back to town with a lighter heart and a plan of action. She would do things her own way and there wasn't a damn thing anyone would be able to do about it.

Roman

Roman gave the punching bag a jab with both fists. He followed that with a fierce kick that left it swinging and rattling on its chain. If he'd dealt that kind of punishment on a human being, they'd be dead or on the way to the emergency room right now. He'd barely slept last night and after tossing and turning for way too long, he finally hit the gym with a vengeance. Roman had planned on spending Sunday in bed and not alone. Instead, he was easing his tensions in the gym.

He'd been too long without a woman and even worse, the only woman he wanted didn't want him. Tossing his boxing gloves to the side, he hit the treadmill. Roman had no idea how many miles he would need to run to rid Madison from his mind but it would never be enough. The whole time he was in Chicago, she was never far from his thoughts. He'd stayed away on purpose but it didn't help. The distance just made him miss her more.

"There you are, boss." Arlo entered the room, a mug in one hand and a pastry in the other.

"Where else would I be?" he snapped. Roman chugged on a bottle of water and wiped his forehead with a nearby towel. Sweat ran down his back.

"Sorry about last night." Arlo leaned against the wall and studied the mug in his hand.

Last night was what he was trying to forget. At

least Arlo had the decency to not look him in the eye.

"What the hell for? It wasn't your fault she left."

It was his. He thought he'd pulled out all the stops, but it wasn't enough.

"I should have checked with you before I took her home."

He threw the now wet towel onto a nearby bench. "It was her choice. I can't make her stay if she doesn't want to."

Arlo halted the cup near his lips. "I don't think I've ever heard of a woman not wanting to stay the night with you. I have to admit it did throw me for a minute when she asked to go home."

"There will be other nights, I can promise you that." He wasn't done with Madison Miller.

"What's on the schedule for today?"

"I haven't decided yet." Love sick fool that he was, he'd planned on spending the day with Madison but things hadn't worked out that way.

"The boys were talking about getting together later to watch the football game." Arlo plopped the last bite of his pastry in his mouth and then wiped his lips with the back of his hand.

"Sounds good. I gave Therese the day off, so why don't you order in and I'll join you."

"Will do, boss." Arlo nodded and left the room.

Roman followed him out and headed for upstairs. Hopefully, a hot shower, and some time with the boys would erase a certain dark haired local from his mind, at least for a little bit.

The hot shower helped, but Madison was still on his mind. Drying off with a heated towel, he suddenly realized he had to go about things a different way. She was someone he couldn't control, that was for sure. Maybe he'd have to let her think she was the one calling the shots.

He laughed at the thought. No, she'd come around. They always did.

Chapter Six

Madison

The store had just opened and Madison wanted to make sure the inventory had been labeled and the gowns were ready for steaming. Thankfully, it would be a quick Saturday with so many things to do in the shop.

"Stephanie?" she called from the back room. "Where are the dresses that came in yesterday?"

"The boxes are behind the new displays. Look to the left." Madison reached out and moved the sturdy metal hanger box that accommodated the rental tuxes. Large brown boxes peeked out. She rearranged the area to get started when the bell over the door rang announcing their first customer of the day.

It'd been almost a week since her date with Roman. He'd called every day asking for a second, but she'd been strong and said no. The man was persistent, that's for sure. He was charming, and way too sexy, a combination that was getting harder and harder to say no to. She wanted a nice family man to settle down with, but being part of a mafia family wasn't a part of her plan, nor was it the kind of household she imagined having.

"Good morning," Madison heard Stephanie saying to a patron. She frowned as she opened the first box of dresses. The way her love life was going, she'd never get to walk down the aisle in one of these stunning gowns.

"Hey! Stop that!" Something crashed in the main shop. "What are you doing?" Stephanie's panic stricken voice sent a shiver down her spine. What in the world? Madison jumped to her feet and rushed out front. A man stood glaring down at Stephanie as his hand sent a rack of dresses tumbling to the floor in a heap of white and tulle.

Oh my God!

"What is going on?" Madison screeched at the top of her lungs at the devastation and the condition of the store. "Who are you?"

The perpetrator didn't speak. He loomed at over six feet and was built like a tank. Instead of acknowledging her, he marched over to the glass display case of crystal jewelry. Seizing a nearby silver candleholder, he smashed it through the glass. Shards of lead crystal flew everywhere like a load of buckshot. Stephanie covered her face with her hand and ducked behind a rack. Next he destroyed the metal veil rack, bending it until it hurtled down into a twisted, splintered wreck. Madison watched in horror as thousands of dollars' worth of her and her mother's inventory was demolished in mere moments.

"Stephanie, call 911," she ordered.

Madison grabbed a nearby cake knife and stepped forward, anger boiling under her skin. "What do you think you're doing?"

He turned to her. His face was void of emotion when he easily disarmed her and used the ribbon decorated knife to slice through a nearby veil.

"This is a message," he finally said in a gruff voice. He walked to the wall and yanked at the rod fastened into the sheet rock. A mess of crumbled wall board littered the area, mixed with the exquisite gowns. Madison screamed at the destruction. Her hands covered her ears and her knees went weak. The intruder stepped closer and she retreated until her back hit the wall. His breath was hot and vile. Beady eyes bore into hers and he pointed a thick tattooed finger in her face. "You'll be hearing from us again and you'd better listen."

The brute retreated, swung on his heel, and left the store. Her heart thumped wildly and tears stung the back of her eyes at the devastation.

Madison dashed to the door, reaching it as soon as it slammed back into its threshold. She twisted the lock, sealing Stephanie and herself inside.

The outline of the man's silhouette strutted down the sidewalk as if he was just out for a stroll.

"They're coming," Stephanie squeaked out on a breath. Blood was all over one side of her face. "The police are coming. They should be here any minute."

"Oh my God. You're hurt."

"It's nothing." Stephanie grabbed a paper towel from the bathroom and held it to her face. They were both in shock. They scanned the room in horror until Madison collapsed on the floor, her head in her hands.

It was bad enough that some madman would cause a mess, but it was only weeks before the event that set the tone for their entire business earnings for the year. *Holy shit*. Who would do this? Why?

***

Madison sat in silence as Stephanie told the police what had happened. At this point, the only simmering memory was of his face—cold, rash, and unrepentant. She wouldn't sleep for weeks after this. Stephanie, *oh God*, she was going to be paranoid and afraid to be here alone. Madison had finally gotten some semblance of security back after her kidnapping, but now the sense of well-being she'd gained as the distance grew after that occurrence had been squashed in a less than a minute. Dim memories of the experience flashed as if it was just yesterday. If not for Roman and his men finding her, she would be dead along with a young bride, and now she'd been vandalized. Nothing like this had ever happened around here and yet she'd been the victim of two crimes in less than a few months.

Three officers roamed her shop, one with a notepad jotting down notes, another photographing the damage, and the last one trying to lift a good fingerprint off some of the items the vandal touched. Insurance would pay for it, but they couldn't erase the scars or the time lost to come back from this. The tightening in her chest slowly crept up to choke her throat. A shortness of breath began to plague her until she was gasping for air.

The ring tone from her phone jarred her from her misery. Stiffened, she followed the sound and found it on the floor behind the counter.

"Hello?"

"Maddy, is that you?" It was Connie, her mother.

"Yes."

"It didn't sound like you. Is everything all right?"

"No. It's not," she sobbed. All heads in the room turned to the entrance as Roman and Arlo entered the shop.

"What's wrong?"

"The shop was just trashed."

"What? What are you talking about, Maddy?" her mother demanded.

"A big thug of a man just walked in the store and started destroying things."

Connie sucked in a sharp gasp. "Is this some kind of a joke?"

"I wish it was." Madison's eyes were locked on Roman's. It was as if he was coming to her rescue again.

"I can't believe it. Are you all right?" Her mother's voice resonated in the background.

Roman briefly studied the damage before walking directly toward her. His face was a dark mask that made her stutter into the phone.

"Yes." Her gaze darted to Stephanie who was now being cared for by first responders. "Stephanie may need stitches. She took some glass to the face."

"What has the world come to?"

"I don't know, *Mom*, maybe if you were here you'd figure it out." She regretted the words as soon as they were uttered.

Roman placed a hand on her shoulder, his face full of concern and bottled up anger.

"Look, Mom, I've got to go."

"But—" It was one of the rare times her mom didn't want to end the conversation first.

"I have to talk to the police. I'll call you later. I need to handle this shit-storm."

"Okay. Call me if you need me." Her voice broke on the word *call*.

"I always need you, Mom." After ending the call, she faced Roman.

"What happened?" Roman stared straight into her eyes. Her nerves screamed at her, not wanting to have to tell the story again.

"I already told the police everything. What are you doing here?" She waved her hand at the disaster surrounding her.

"I heard and came right over. Have you ever seen this guy before?" His eyes flashed. "Do you know what he wanted?"

"A guy came in and destroyed the place. That's it. I don't know who the hell he was or what the hell he was thinking."

More questions she'd already answered and the questions were coming from Roman, of all people. Madison reached down to pull a tiara out of the wreckage, shaking it off. Inside, she was crying.

"He said it was a message." Madison spoke

through the lump in the back of her throat, her gaze fixed on the glittering bent crown.

Roman raised an eyebrow and folded his arms across his chest. "What kind of message?"

"That I'd be hearing from him again and I'd better listen." The threat didn't make sense. The whole episode didn't make sense. She didn't have any competitors for miles and no one she could think of would want to do her harm.

One of the taller police officers walked over.

"Roman." The men shook hands.

"Ry, what can you tell me about who did this?"

"Wait, you two know each other?" Madison interrupted, suspicious that the mafia and the cops had congenial conversations.

"We've known each other since we were kids," Officer Ryan Donavan said. "We were on the high school football team."

The day was getting stranger and stranger with every passing minute.

"An unknown suspect ransacked the place and threatened the staff. I sent one of my guys out to question anybody in the area who might have witnessed the guy leaving. It's early and the shops are opening up or don't open for another hour. Whoever did this planned it right." Officer Donavan gazed around. "We lifted a few prints. Hopefully he's in the system. As soon as we get any further info, I'll let you know." Madison stewed. This was her place. Her shock now turned to outrage.

"Thanks, Ry. The sooner the better."

"We'll do what we can." Officer Donavan handed her his card. "I think we got everything. If you think of anything else, please call. Any details will help us catch the perpetrator." He then stopped to talk to Stephanie one more time and left her with a card as well. The ruckus of officers and onlookers departed as quickly as they came.

Roman strolled over to the metal rack that had been twisted into a pretzel.

"Arlo."

"Yeah?"

"Call Dominic. Tell him to get the hell over here and see what he can do to fix this shit."

"Right, boss."

"And take photos. The insurance company is going to want them."

"I'm on it," Arlo said and pulled his cell from his pocket.

She hated to admit it, but it felt good to have him here. It felt good to have someone take charge for once instead of her, but it was still her store.

"I've got a guy," Roman said. "He'll get these displays back together in no time."

"Thanks." On shaky legs, she staggered over and gathered Stephanie in her arms. "But I'm all set. I can handle this." The bleeding cut on Stephanie's face had slowed down but it was deep. She was definitely taking her to the hospital to get checked out. Why her friend refused to go with the medics was beyond her. They even had her sign a form that Steph had declined further treatment.

"I won't take no for an answer." He clenched his fists, obviously annoyed with her resistance. A 'don't argue with me' look was clearly written on his face.

Madison dismissed the comment. She'd had enough of being bullied by men for one day and her immediate concern was her friend. "I'm taking Steph to the ER. You can stay or go."

Roman crossed his arms in front of his chest.

"Let's go, Steph."

"I'm not going, and that's that." Stephanie was obviously in pain, but Madison didn't want to argue with her any further. All this turmoil was giving her a headache.

She grabbed a black sharpie pen and a white piece of paper from the copy machine. Writing in sharp, frantic lettering, she made a sign:

Closed until further notice.

Chapter Seven

Roman

Roman frowned. He'd never met a more stubborn woman in his life. Correction, make that *two* stubborn women. The fact that Stephanie refused to go to the hospital, but agreed to see the Caponelli family's private physician set off a red flag.

"Arlo. Get some guys to shadow them. I want a tail on them at all times."

"I'm on it." He took out his cell and made a few calls.

He stretched his fingers out of the tight fist he'd been holding and studied the disarray of the shop. Diego's men were the only ones to come to mind. This type of shit was their style. A bridal shop? "Fucking losers," he cursed. A smirk touched the corners of Roman's mouth and the glory of *offing* Diego spread across his lips. Killing him left no remorse. The guy was an asshole. Any acquaintances of his were probably still toasting his demise and far from here.

It had to be an outsider, someone moving in on Genoa. Roman swore under his breath. This was his territory and no one else's. Arlo would have to do some digging.

"Hey, boss." Arlo stepped to his side, a scowl on his face.

"Yeah?"

"The men are in place and Dom's on his way." Dominic was a cleaner in more ways than one. The guy had a tragic past, but seemed to fit in perfectly with the family. He was a gifted artist who could weld or make anything out of iron and metals. Dom was equally creative at torture and disposing of bodies. He was a fucking artist in all things. What Roman liked best about the man was that he never questioned an order and didn't talk much.

"Good." Roman puffed out his cheeks.

Fury raised its ugly head again as he surveyed all the damage that had been done to the store. If the fucker who did this had touched Madison, he'd have skinned him alive. Roman had to squeeze his eyes shut, the idea hurt so badly.

"You stay until he gets here. Have him fix or replace anything that's broken. Then meet up with me." The urge to bang some heads together was overwhelming. "I'm going to the cop shop. See if they found out anything new. You make some calls too. Find out if anyone knows who this prick is."

"What do you want done with him when we find him?" That's one of the things he liked best about his friend. It wasn't *if* they found him but *when* they found him. Arlo was a bloodhound. The guy had already taken a seat in one of the shop's sofa chairs that hadn't been vandalized and began to flick through his contact list.

"Just find him. I don't just want to know who, I want to know why." With that, he left the shop, the bell jingling over his head, and went straight to the police station.

Visiting the Genoa Police Department was not what he'd had on his schedule for the day, but the sooner he found out what he was dealing with, the better.

His shoes echoed on the shiny tile of the department floors as he found his way to Ryan Donavan's office. They'd gone to the same school as kids and even hung out together after class. They were friends, plain and simple. When they each followed in the footsteps of their fathers, things seemed to fall apart. Roman and Ryan had each other's back on and off the football field, but since graduation they had gone their separate ways, which, considering their professions, made sense.

Never in his wildest dreams did he expect to end up in the same town where Ryan was a local police officer. He still considered him a friend and Ry had been very beneficial in helping with the mess with Diego, but he had to be careful to not expect or ask too much. The guy had a job to do and their friendship was a conflict of interest.

Roman knocked twice on the opened office door before stepping in and making himself comfortable in the chair in front of one Genoa PD's finest. Officer Donavan was on the phone but nodded when he entered the room. Ending the call, Ryan tossed the phone on his desk and leaned back in his chair.

"Caponelli," Ryan said.

"What have you got on the man who ransacked Bell and Bows?" Roman rested his hand on Ryan's desk.

"We sent the prints into the state crime lab, but don't hold your breath waiting for the results."

"Why the hell is that?" Roman tapped his index finger on the desk.

"Cut backs, backlog, take your pick. Unless someone is murdered, the prints go to the back of the line." Ryan was all business.

"Fuck. Don't you have any connections there?" Roman crossed his leg over his knee and rested his elbow on the arm of the chair. "Someone who could, say, move it to the front of the line?"

"I wish. That would make my job a lot easier, but no, I don't. Even if I did, we are looking at vandalism. Depending on the damage done, we're looking at a misdemeanor at best."

"The women could have been hurt." Roman beat his fist on the desk. "My woman could have been hurt."

Ryan raised an eyebrow as he leaned forward.

Madison wasn't his woman, yet. It drove him insane some days, but she would be his.

"I don't care what you have to do, but get me this guy's name," Roman growled.

"And then what?" Ryan frowned.

"You let me worry about that."

"Look, I could give a shit about dirt bags like Diego, but I don't want bodies piling up in my town. It's bad for the town and bad for the businesses."

"Letting scum like this trash the town is worse."

Ryan exhaled loudly. "Miss Miller mentioned the guy had some tattoos on his fingers."

Roman shrugged his shoulders, leaning back in the chair. "Doesn't seem typical of any gang members I know of or rival families."

"The whole thing…it sounds personal. Does she have any enemies that you know of?" Ryan grabbed a notepad and pen.

"No."

"Could it be that someone is sending *you* a message and not her?" Ryan gave Roman a knowing look. "Word gets around. You're not playing with her, are you?"

Roman grimaced. "I'm not fucking playing a game with her."

"Yeah, okay…Romeo."

"If you weren't a cop, I would fucking punch you in the face right now."

Ryan roared with laughter. "Wow, you've got it bad."

Roman stood and glared. "Just figure this shit out." He turned and left the station more annoyed and agitated than when he got there.

If someone was harassing Madison because of him, the death toll in Genoa would be on the rise very shortly. Screw Ryan and his bad for business shit.

Roman's phone buzzed. Arlo was on the other end. "Tell me you have news."

"No. But Dom is working a fucking miracle in

the shop."

Another call came through. Valentina. "I gotta go." Roman switched over.

"I heard about Madison's shop. Is she okay?"

"Yeah. Her friend had some cuts, though."

"I don't like this, Roman." Valentina's voice was low. "This smells like a turf war."

"What?" Valentina had the uncanny ability to see through motivations. That was mostly the reason why she was in law school. She had a gift.

"Who the fuck wants a turf war in Genoa? And why?" he spat.

"That's what you have to figure out." Valentina became quiet.

"Your mind is going a mile a minute. Spit it out," Roman barked.

"Come on, Roman. The deal with Diego and now this."

Roman felt he had chosen well. Genoa was an affluent low crime area. What he did flew under the radar and he kept his business quiet and took most of it elsewhere. His father ran most of the illegal stuff out of Chicago.

"Maybe you brought this on," she said.

"Me? You are fucking saying this is my fault?"

"Yeah, I am." Valentina blew a breath into the phone. "I'm going to see if I can get Madison to stay with me for a while until you sort this out."

That pissed Roman off even more. If anyone was going to protect Madison, it was going to be him.

"I'll talk to you later." He clipped the end button and called Arlo back.

"Pick her up," he ordered into the phone.

"Come again?" Arlo said.

"When you're done, pick Madison up and take her to my house."

"I don't think she is going to come willingly, Boss."

"And there's a problem with that?"

Arlo sighed. "Okay."

"You handle it, personally. I don't want anyone else touching her."

"Got it."

"Good. I have some calls to make."

Madison

The tub Madison soaked in was fragrant, steamy, and just what the doctor ordered after the horrific day she'd had. She took the last sip of Moscato and set the glass on the bathroom floor. It was her second one. Taking a deep breath, she sank a little lower in the tub. The scent of the eucalyptus spearmint body wash her mother had picked up for her during one of her travels soaked through her skin and helped clear her mind. Damn, in all the chaos she'd forgotten to call her mother back.

After dropping Stephanie off at her house and making sure she'd laid down to rest, Madison broke every speed limit to get home. Thankfully, some stitches from the doc and a pill to help her sleep were all that Stephanie needed to get her through the night after their traumatic day.

No longer having to put on a brave face, she let the tears flow. She hadn't sobbed like that in years and once they started, they didn't stop. Her tears mixed with the sudsy bathwater. Crying hard, Madison could taste the salt of her sobbing. She smacked her fist against the porcelain tub before truly gaining her composure. She'd hoped to go back to the bridal shop, maybe try to clean up the mess, but it was too soon. Madison knew her limits. It would be stupid to tackle it when her emotions ran so high.

Her phone buzzed with a call and her gaze shot to the rectangular electronic device gently bouncing on the tile. The word *Mom* lit up with her mother's youthful face. Madison would be lucky to get her genes. Her mother always looked a decade below her true age. If Connie was only concerned with the state of the business, she could wait. She let it go, the phone dancing around until it finally stopped.

Madison pressed the tip of her sudsy finger on her iPad to play her favorite tunes to chill with. The music instantly filled the bathroom and she let her head rest comfortably on the cushioned bath pillow. It was a luxury that was now a necessity. The combination of the day's events and the horror she endured a few months ago created a mantra of *everything will work out* and *everything will be fine*. Scarlett O'Hara's *tomorrow is another day* repeated in Madison's mind while her eyes closed.

She slipped lower in the bubbles, trying to block out the world, just her nose, ears, and forehead peeking out. It worked. Little by little, her neck and shoulders loosened, and calm began to settle in her twisted stomach which she'd been certain would be permanently filled with acidic bile.

A bump sounded from the living room, not loud

or alarming but curious. Madison froze and her heart rate somersaulted. She listened long and hard. Nothing. It was probably her older home's moans and groans as the evening chill settled in. The sounds she never noticed until she was alone at night. Willing herself to relax, she closed her eyes.

A tiny shuffle came from outside the bathroom door and Madison's eyes snapped open. It stopped, but that didn't alleviate the racing of her heart at the minor noise. She listened intently for a long, stretched moment. Nothing. Her heartbeat steadied and she went back to soaking and washing away the dreadful day. Other inhabitants could be heard through the walls at times. It was probably just a field mouse seeking warmth in the walls on a cold night. Rationalizing away the thousands of reasons for bumps and bangs was easier than investigating to only find out it was nothing. Being jumpy was probably a common thing after such an ordeal. The water had soothed away the stress and Madison was not giving up on the pleasantness. It was not in her nature. Minutes slipped into at least thirty.

A knock on her bathroom door made her jump a mile, sloshing the foamy water on the floor and on her phone. The device lifted and slid too far away to reach.

"Madison? It's Arlo."

"What the hell are you doing in my house?" she screamed. Sheer vehemence sucked its way through Madison. She'd been violated already today, and now her sanctuary was breached by one of Roman's henchmen. "Get out of my house before I call the cops."

"I'm not leaving until you come out."

"How did you get in?" There was no way she'd left the front door unlocked after what happened. It had taken everything she had not to give in to the urge to push the couch in front of the door.

"I told you." His voice traveled through the door. "It's easy to get in this place. You need better locks and a security system."

She'd never had any problems before. "What. Do. You. Want?" Madison stayed right in her tub. This was her home. How dare he come in unannounced?

"Um. I've come to get you."

"Get me? What the hell does that mean?"

"Roman…he wants you to come to stay…at *his* house."

"Are you out of your mind? I live here. I'm staying here. You. Leave. Now. And lock up when you go."

Madison crossed her arms over her naked breasts. If Arlo could break into her home so easily, nothing could stop him from coming through her thin, unlocked, bathroom door. She quickly reached for the fluffy gold towel on the hook next to her.

"I know you're in the tub. I really think you should put something on and hurry. He doesn't like to wait. Roman wants you at his house. It's safer."

"From what?" Madison tossed back.

Whispery voices emanated from her living room. *Shit. Are more people out there?* The tears threatened to spring again. The face of the asshole from earlier flashed across her mind, causing her heart to catapult in fear.

"I told you." A warning echoed through the door. Fear of what was going on made her move. Madison stood and wrapped the towel around herself while lunging for the door knob, practically slipping on the tile to twist the lock.

"You've got two seconds to get out or I'm calling the police. I've got my phone in here."

The bang of someone's shoulder bounced off the archaic door. Its antique lock rattled on the hinges.

"Ahhhhh." Madison screamed. "Go away."

Bang. A shoulder hit the door again, and the wood bent against the weight. Splinters flew in several directions. Madison backed away and retreated to a corner.

Bang number three completed the mission. The door burst open. Fractured wood was everywhere. Her home was now in shambles. She trembled between the tub and the sink, dripping water on the floor while wrapped only in a towel.

But it wasn't Arlo who hovered in the doorway, eyes blazing.

It was Roman.

Chapter Eight

Roman

Madison wearing nothing but a towel was not what he'd been expecting to find when he walked through the door of her house and barged into her bathroom. Her thick hair had been up in the back. Loose curly strands gently framed her face. A girly fragrance floated in the air. Her golden skin was still damp from her bath and dewy drops of water streamed down in areas not yet touched by the towel she gripped tightly. So tight, in fact, that her breasts threatened to spill over the top. He knew she had long legs but never dreamed they would be this shapely. Even her toes were sexy, red polish dotting the ends. Growing aroused, he knew he needed to leave, now.

Arlo was supposed to have had her packed, ready to go, and out of here. Instead he decided to pack her things first. Give her time to finish her bath, Arlo had explained, trying to ease the tension. He knew Roman would be pissed as shit when he had to come out here.

Hell, he didn't have time for this. She was a distraction and one he couldn't afford. He was going to keep her safe and find out who was behind the destruction of her shop. Or the bigger picture in the scheme of things, find out who might be moving into their territory.

Roman wanted her, needed her, but it was not the time for that. Things had been so much simpler when they first met last fall. It was important to keep his head in the game. Making her his own would have to wait.

"Get dressed now." It was best to remain angry at her right now, but desire and possession overtook him. He wanted her and damn everything else to hell. His fingers itched to rip the towel from her body. Roman had to get out of here before he took her slippery and wet up against the bathroom wall. That was definitely not how he wanted their first time together to be.

"Don't order me around. Get out of my house." Her deep blue eyes were wide and her cheeks pink and flushed. He secretly hoped it was because of him and not her recent soak in the tub.

"You're coming with me." He stepped out of the bathroom to address Arlo and gain relief from the tightening in his pants.

"Do you have her things packed yet?" he barked.

Arlo stood perplexed in front of her closet, a sweater in one hand and a pair of sweatpants in the other. If Roman wasn't in such a hurry, the sight of Arlo trying to figure out what to put in her suitcase would have had him bent over in laughter, but this was serious and knowing Madison was only in a towel in the next room made him hot all over again.

"Uh, it might be best if she picked out her own stuff." His best friend had never looked so stressed.

Poking his head back into the bathroom, he narrowly missed being beamed by a roll of toilet paper. Madison still hadn't moved. "That's all you've got, sweetheart?" He smirked and leaned against the broken door frame.

"Get out." She screamed and whipped a jar of lotion at his head. This time, he wasn't as fast. The container cracked him right on the bone below his eye. That would surely leave a mark. He raised his fingers to his now throbbing cheek. Damn, that hurt.

Roman exhaled, feeling his cheekbone throb and counted to ten in his head. Wandering back in her bedroom, he spied a robe on the bed. Determined, he grabbed the robe and headed to the bathroom for the last time.

"You have two choices. Either put on this robe or keep the towel. One way or the other, you are leaving with me in ten seconds." His eyes narrowed. "You decide."

Madison stepped closer, reaching cautiously for the robe. Finally, he breathed a sigh of relief.

Suddenly, everything went black. *What the hell?* Roman was blinded by soft fleece and small hands thrust at his chest. Madison had thrown the robe over his head and pushed. His shoes slipped on the water soaked floor and he fell back against the tub just narrowly missing landing in the water. "Son of a…" He cursed, flinging the robe from his head.

"Arlo, grab her." Roman's voice was at an

ominous low.

Regaining his feet, Roman rushed after her. Arlo had her by the arm, stopping her. There was no escape now.

"Put her things in the car. We'll be right out," Roman snapped.

Arlo, happy to get the hell out of there, released her, grabbed her haphazardly filled bags, and left the room in a hurry.

Madison stood proudly before Roman, smug and defiant. She wasn't giving an inch, and he couldn't help but admire her will.

He held the robe out one last time. "Like I said, we are leaving, so wear this or go naked. I don't care."

In a stunning display of defiance, the beautiful woman in front of him narrowed her eyes. Dramatically, she dropped the towel. His heart stopped and the front of his pants constricted again. She snatched the forgotten garment from his hands and quickly donned the robe.

With a determined glare on her face, she stomped her foot then folded her arms across her chest.

"I'm not going anywhere. This is my home. I've been bullied enough for one day."

Roman chuckled and wished she'd kept the robe off. In a swoop, he bent down and tossed her over his shoulder, fireman style. Madison squealed and kicked with her feet.

"You can have your way some other day, but right now, like it or not, you're coming with me."

"Put me down," Madison screamed.

"Not today, sweetheart."

"This is kidnapping," she cried. "You're no better than Diego. I thought you were different."

That comment cut like a knife to his heart. They were nothing alike. Diego was a vicious abuser of women. Roman stopped at the front door and set her on her feet. He kept both hands on her forearms to keep her immobile.

"You're coming with me. Now, you can either have your neighbors see you be carried out over my shoulder or you can come willingly."

She opened her mouth but he stopped her with a gentle tap to her lips with his finger. "I'm trying to protect you. The person who trashed your business and threatened you may come after you again. This is for your own good." Her eyes misted and his heart ached to pull her into his arms and promise that everything would be okay. "Are you willing to take that chance?"

Madison wiped her eyes with the back of her hand.

"What's it going to be?" He had her backed into a corner figuratively. Madison looked torn.

She stomped over to the closet and flung open the door. She mumbled under her breath, but he couldn't make out what was uttered. As she threw on a coat and slipped on a pair of Uggs, he thought he made out a word or two, *bastard, asshole*. He'd been called worse, but hearing it from Madison's pretty bowed lips stung like hell.

Chapter Nine

Madison

Madison yawned and stretched her arms in the air. Snuggling into the pillow under her head, she refused to open her eyes. It was Sunday. There was no need to hit the alarm clock and go to work. Maybe she'd take a walk later, get some fresh air, and even stop at the Java Shop for an espresso. Oh, and that cake she loved. But the bliss was erased and morphed into a mess when everything came flooding back to her. Stephanie, the shop, and Roman snatching her from her own home. What a mess.

Opening her eyes, she took in the opulent surroundings and groaned. She'd been infuriated last night.

Stupid!

Stupid!

Stupid!

Madison had flashed Roman her body out of spite. Again, she gauged the finery in the guest room of Roman's lakeside home. She hadn't agreed to come here. It was all force.

She sat up with a start and padded to the door to her temporary room. Someone was rummaging around in the kitchen. Cupboard doors opened and closed. The refrigerator door suctioned shut. Some coffee beans zipped and pulverized in a grinder. Soon the crack of an egg echoed before it sizzled in a warm pan.

All the welcoming sounds of an ordinary kitchen, only there was nothing commonplace about this house. Madison glanced to where she'd rested her head for the last few hours. She hadn't drooled and there were no mascara marks marring the gazillion thread count pillow case. The two doors across from her room were for the en suite bathroom and closet. Needing to use the facilities and clean up her face, she made her way there.

Madison showered and looked for the luggage Arlo supposedly packed during the drama at her house last night. It was nowhere to be found in the room. *Great.* She spied the closet door and peeked inside. Her jaw fell open. From floor to ceiling, it was jammed packed with dresses, shoes, hats, coats, and Madison's own clothes from her home. It made her stew inside. Apparently, Roman was always fully stocked for female company.

She grabbed a pair of jeans and a sweater she knew was hers and put them on, shoving down the thoughts of the amount of women that may have slept in this room or his. Slamming the door behind her, she fled to the cozy sounds coming from the nearby room, her stomach growling the whole way.

In the kitchen, she saw a perfectly shaped plump bottom poking out while rummaging in the refrigerator. Bacon sizzled on the stove. Popping up and putting butter on the counter was Valentina. She spun when she noticed Madison in her periphery.

"Oh my God." She threw her arms around Madison. "Are you okay? I heard all about what happened. You must have been so scared." Madison had trouble getting a word out as Valentina gushed. "Are you hungry? Would you like some coffee? Juice?"

It warmed her to receive a welcome and she felt guilty for her thoughts as she rummaged through the closet. The clothes and the room she slept in last night must have belonged to Valentina. Madison knew she spent a great deal of time here.

"I'm fine and yes, I'm starving." Madison smiled. Valentina was infectious. It was impossible not to like her.

"Good morning," Roman said from the doorway of the kitchen. Jeans and a well-worn t-shirt hugged his body. He strode forward and gave each of them a peck on the cheek like this was a typical everyday family moment. Madison swore his kiss rested a moment longer than the one he gave Valentina. The contact sent chills down her spine. Damn him and the way he made her stomach flutter.

Valentina set out placemats on the granite counter, each one in front of a stool. Roman's phone buzzed.

"Excuse me," he said while walking toward the wall of windows.

"Sit," Valentina ordered.

"Can I help with anything?"

"No, you're a guest. Sit." She poured a cup of coffee and set it on a saucer.

Madison sat down in front of the mug with awareness to everywhere Roman paced behind her in the open floor plan.

"I'm handling it. I will find out…" There was a long pause and his voice dropped menacingly low. "I've told you before, I'm not doing it. This isn't the dark ages…. I understand, but you have to respect my wishes. This is my life we're talking about and I won't forfeit it for something that should have been done a long time ago." Roman flexed his free hand as he paced. "No, and that's final." The conversation cut off and Madison noticed Valentina stiffened as she worked. A plate of hot eggs and bacon was placed in front of her.

"Would you like some juice?" Valentina smiled at her but it didn't reach her eyes.

"That would be great." Madison answered nonchalantly, but her thoughts were still on the conversation Roman had with the mystery caller.

He tossed the phone on the counter and took the seat next to her.

"Oh no," Madison blurted out.

"What's wrong?" He turned her way.

"I just remembered my phone. I think it's still floating in water on my bathroom floor." She needed to check on Stephanie and see how she was doing. Not to mention, let her know where she was. Hopefully, her phone and iPad were still in good working order. If not, she'd be sending Roman the bill.

"Arlo will be here any minute with it and some coffee." He rose, grabbed both their coffee mugs and poured the liquid in the sink. Valentina folded her arms across her chest and her lower lip poked out.

"I love you, Valentina, and you're a great cook, but your coffee always tastes like shit." Roman gazed lovingly at his sister even when insulting her. He valued his family. A ping of jealousy ripped through Madison's chest. She didn't have a relationship like the one Roman and Valentina shared with anyone in her family. Her mother was absent eight months a year.

The doorbell chimed. Valentina rattled off what sounded like displeasure in Italian and leaped to go answer it.

"That was rude," Madison chastised.

Roman shrugged his shoulders. "Feel free to try it, but don't say I didn't warn you."

Madison was determined to not disappoint her friend. Heading over to the coffee pot with purpose and a mug in hand, she changed her mind after getting a whiff of what was brewing.

"What is that stench?" The comment should have been limited to her thoughts. It smelled rancid but had just been brewed. Sheepishly, Madison returned to her seat.

Roman laughed. "The food's safe to eat." He had already dug into the bacon and eggs.

She slid her chair over. His pine aftershave enticed her nearer, but it was too intimate sitting so close. The whole kitchen scene brought back memories of their previous dinner here, the one that was supposed to have included Valentina. Only this time the jerk had kidnapped her, for crying out loud. He was brutish and controlling at times.

The attempt at space didn't work. The legs of her stool screeched as he reached for her chair and slid her back to the original spot.

"I like you close," he confessed, unashamed.

Twisting in her seat, Madison prepared to do battle. Her mouth opened but nothing came out. Judging by his body language, this was not the time to start an argument. And she softened at the gesture of pulling her close. He was obviously troubled about something, not to mention the black eye he was sporting.

"Did I do that?" She cringed, reliving the moment she threw the lotion jar.

"Do what?" Roman raised the eyebrow over the one that had been hit.

Meekly, she pointed to his injury.

"This? It's nothing." She must not have appeared convinced because he kept talking. "I've been shot, stabbed, clubbed over the head." He dug into his food again. "It takes more than a jar of cold cream to put a dent in me."

"Body lotion."

"What?" He was definitely distracted by something.

"It was a jar of body lotion."

He reached over and squeezed her hand briefly with a smile that reached all the way to his eyes before returning his attention to their breakfast.

"You should eat, sweetheart."

Reluctantly, she picked up her fork. This was by far the oddest meal she'd ever had. Madison had been prepared to give him a piece of her mind, but common sense told her this was not the time or place. As much as she hated to admit it, a small part of her was enjoying it.

Valentina soon returned followed by Arlo. She didn't appear to be as upset as when she'd left.

She held a box of pastries from their favorite coffee shop and Arlo followed with a carrier filled with four containers of coffee and a thermos of more under his arm. The heady aroma perked Madison up for the first time that day. It was on the tip of her tongue to sing a *thank you* song when a cup of espresso was placed in front of her.

"What's the news?" Roman flicked through some messages on his phone while he talked to Arlo.

"Nothing yet. No one seems to know anything about the guy." Valentina placed a heaping plate of food in front of him and he eagerly dug in. As he shoved food into his mouth, he retrieved a phone from his pocket and set it in front of Madison.

"Thank you." She picked it up. The screen was black.

"Maybe the rice trick will work," Valentina offered as she stared over Madison's shoulder at the lifeless phone. "Here, give it to me."

"Dammit. What the hell is going on?" Roman cursed and pushed his now empty plate away. "Get someone to start checking on any new acquisitions in town. Homes, businesses, I don't give a damn. I want to know about any new people moving in here.

I don't care if they're a Priest or citizen of the year. I want names."

Valentina and Madison listened while she submerged her phone into a big bowl of uncooked white rice.

"I'm on it. As soon as I finish this delicious meal." Arlo winked at Valentina, who in turn smiled and wrinkled her nose at Roman. They were so brother and sister.

"Valentina, you help too. Search for any recent crimes in the area and see if there have been any other attacks or similar incidences."

Arlo's phone buzzed and he took a glance. "Speaking of crime, Donavan is at the front gates."

"Maybe he has something useful." Roman sighed and ran his fingers threw his hair.

"Only one way to find out." His right hand man left to go greet their uninvited guest.

Madison sat quietly, but her mind wasn't. It wouldn't hurt to stay here a little longer until she knew what was going on. Did it mean she wasn't still mad as hell at Mr. tall, dark, and mobster? Oh, hell no, but she would just let it go for the time being.

The kitchen had become a busy place. Arlo returned followed by the slim cut, black haired officer of the Genoa police force. Madison remembered seeing him in town many times. Everyone knew who everyone was even if they didn't know each other personally.

"Morning, Donavan." Roman rose and shook his hand.

"Morning. I'm sorry to interrupt your meal, but

I'm following up on a call this morning." Officer Donavan retrieved a small notebook from his shirt pocket. "Seems a neighbor of Miss Miller's saw her leave last night with some men in a black SUV, but she never returned. The concerned neighbor noticed men going in and out of her home this morning. When she phoned Miss Miller and received no answer, the neighbor placed a call to our department."

Madison shrank back in her seat, shocked.

"What?" Had her home been ransacked too?

"I thought I would stop by and see if you knew anything about it." The officer looked directly at Madison. "I'm so glad to see you're in good health, Miss Miller. Would you mind telling me what's going on?"

Before she could, Roman stood up.

"I was concerned about Madison staying home alone with an unknown perpetrator lurking around. I've welcomed her to stay here with myself and my sister." He motioned to Valentina, whose cheeks were a bright pink ever since the handsome police officer walked in the room. "I also hired some guys to update the locks and install a security system at both her home and business. I won't be comfortable until the man is apprehended...or *taken care of*."

What 'taken care of' meant, Madison knew exactly. A shudder ran through her along with a second one that rattled her mind. She couldn't afford a security system.

"Is that correct, Miss Miller?" Officer Donavan addressed her, but she wasn't sure what to say. It was her chance to leave of her own free will, but then what? Roman seemed to think there was a threat against her. When the face of the criminal who'd trashed her shop flashed before her eyes, she sucked in a breath and released it with, "Yes, that's correct," on her lips.

Donavan's blue eyes studied her for a moment before digging in his pocket for a card. Handing one to her, he said, "If you need anything, anything at all, don't hesitate to call."

The card read *Officer Ryan Donavan* and listed his phone number and the address of the Genoa Police Department. "I will. Thank you."

"Thanks for stopping in, Ry." Roman shook his hand.

Valentina suddenly spoke. "Hello, Ryan."

Ryan addressed Valentina, seeming to see her for the first time. "It's been a long time." His voice had an added swagger to its intonation.

"Yes." Her voice sounded higher than normal.

He took a step in her direction. "You look great. All grown up."

That seemed to get a rise out of her and she stood up. "I'm not so little anymore."

Madison watched with amusement as Ryan's gaze swept her from head to toe, causing Valentina to blush even more.

Donavan slipped another card out of his pocket and handed it her way. "In case you have need of my services, as well…."

"I'm sure that won't be necessary," Roman said. She dismissed him and crossed her arms over her chest.

"Roman, Miss Miller." Ryan nodded.

"Valentina, it's a pleasure to see you again." Officer Donavan left, following Arlo out of the room.

Valentina fingered the business card, took a long stare at it and then turned to leave.

"Where are you going?" Roman asked.

"To get started on tracking these dirt bags down," she retorted before leaving the room. "And," she pointed to Madison. "Don't think I have forgotten about your show. Everything will get done. Don't worry."

Silence filled the room in her absence. The seriousness of the situation finally settled on her shoulders. Roman wasn't just doing this to make her stay. He was doing it to keep her safe.

Chapter Ten

Roman

Roman hated fucking bad feelings. He sensed Valentina was a little too enthusiastic about seeing Ryan, and Pop had just ruined his breakfast with the one person in the world he wanted to spend time with, Madison. This wasn't the dark ages and if Pop thought he would succumb to his arrangement of marriage to Layla Rinaldi, he was mistaken. Roman had come far in his thirty years, and wouldn't be told who to marry.

Roman glanced at Madison, who'd poured her third cup of coffee from the thermos and currently had both her hands wrapped around the warm mug. He couldn't help but be elated that she was here. It was bullshit what happened to her place, but it made for a fortuitous situation for him. Selfishly, this was his chance to win her over and keep her within arm's reach.

Rising from the kitchen counter, Roman

retrieved a laptop with one hand that had been lying on a side table.

"Here." He placed it in front of her. "You need to replace the gowns that were damaged. That event is going to be here soon. You need to be ready for it."

Madison stared down at the search engine in awe.

Roman placed an American Express card in front of her. "Order whatever you want. I've got it. The shop is being worked on as we speak. You should be up and running in a week." *That should give me plenty of time*, he thought to himself.

"I can't take your money. It'll cost a ton to replace those dresses and accessories."

Roman shrugged. "It's not a concern. Spend what you need to."

Gauging the look on Madison's face, he wasn't sure if she was horrified, stunned, or grateful. Damn, he didn't understand women sometimes. Then an amazing thing happened. Her face softened and she seemed appreciative.

"I'll pay you back as soon as we collect the insurance money. The shop needs to get back on its feet. But…I *will* pay you back." Her voice was soft and hinted of defeat. Roman didn't like it. His spit-fire Madison wasn't shooting daggers at him or refusing to comply. But this softer side had its appeal too. He couldn't help himself. She was too tempting. Madison began typing away to her suppliers and Roman risked it. He wrapped his arm around her shoulder, pulled her in slightly, and kissed the top of her head.

"Anything for you," he whispered before he snatched his cell phone off the counter and went to his office to work on other problems.

Madison

Madison held the credit card in her hand and spun it around as she sat at the counter. Royal Distributor's website lit up on the laptop screen that Roman loaned her. The company was her largest supplier of gowns, so hopefully they could replenish her stock quickly. She wrestled with the situation. He'd given her his credit card to restock her shop. He was right. If she didn't order what she needed now, it would never be delivered in time for the bridal show. Time was not in her favor. Madison remembered every gown she had ever sold or bought. The image of the destroyed dresses, veils, and jewelry snapped across her mind including the man's face who'd violated her place of business and hurt her friend. A tickle of fear crept up her back. Nothing made sense.

She hadn't done anything to anyone to spark such a horrific retaliation. Her competition was practically non-existent in Genoa. There had to be something going on that would reach the surface of explanation at some point.

Beep. Beep. Beep. Madison looked around the kitchen at the empty plates, the refrigerator, and her face twisted in confusion. She rose from her stool and walked around the counter. The sound was coming from the big bowl of rice.

My phone.

It worked. Madison dug her fingers into the tiny white oblong bits and rescued the cell. The screen lit up with voicemails, texts, and missed calls. Four of them had been from her mother. Ignoring those, she scrolled directly to Stephanie's texts.

Where are you?

Call me.

What is happening?

Madison texted immediately, seeing that those texts were hours old.

At Roman's. I'm fine. Working on getting the shop back to normal. How are you feeling?

Stephanie: YOU ARE AT ROMAN'S?

All caps, not a good sign.

Before she could text back, her phone rang. Stephanie.

"Hello," Madison said into the receiver.

"Why are you at Roman's?"

"It's a long story. How are you feeling after yesterday? Are you okay?"

"I feel much better. Now tell me why you're at Roman's."

"Well…" Madison recalled being forced to come, but didn't want Stephanie to worry. "Roman felt it is safer for me here after what happened."

"I went to the shop when I didn't hear from you.

I got worried," Stephanie admitted. "It's practically all fixed."

"Fixed? I haven't even called the insurance company. That was next on my list of things to do."

"There were workers there. Putting stuff back together, throwing trash into a dumpster outside, vacuuming up the glass. I even saw new display racks still wrapped in plastic. I couldn't find you, so I left. I thought you knew."

"Stephanie, I have to call you back."

Madison pressed the end button and dropped her phone back in the rice with a splat. A few nuggets of rice spilled over the side. Her stocking feet took her on a trek through the Caponelli mansion. A door halfway down the hallway was ajar. The deep tone of Roman's voice carried into the hall as she approached. The urge to eavesdrop was strong.

"The sales have to be related to what happened at Madison's. I want a meeting." Menace coated his words. "Tomorrow." He stopped talking, so she assumed he ended the call without a goodbye.

Madison planted her palm against the paneled door and pushed slightly. The movement of the door revealed a very distinguished Roman seated behind an opulent desk scattered with stacks of papers and a mug filled with hot coffee. His chin leaned on his hand, but Madison's intrusion yanked him from his thoughts.

She was confused, and hit a crossroad. Madison never wanted to be beholden to any man, but she hated to admit that she needed Roman. That she enjoyed needing him. He took her independence away, he took her from her home, but the considerate and thoughtful things melted her. She stood in the doorway and their eyes met. The words she wanted to speak were suddenly missing. His eyes said more than any of her words ever could. She could see deep within them. His advances, gifts, and his help weren't because he needed another conquest. He did them because he actually cared.

"Boss," Arlo called from the other side of the house. "Boss."

Roman rose, never removing his gaze from Madison. She stepped aside to let him by, but he stopped for a moment and kissed her forehead similarly to the way he'd done an hour ago. No strings, no seduction, just an unsaid promise.

"Roman. We have company."

Chapter Eleven

Madison

Her skin still tingled on the spot his lips touched. The man could melt ice in the Arctic he was so hot. She trailed behind like a lovesick puppy. It was happening again. There was something about him that pulled to her, urged her to be closer like when they'd first met.

Ahead, a woman's voice could be heard in a heated exchange. This was a busy place today. Madison couldn't see who it was yet, but whoever it was, she certainly didn't seem happy.

The door burst open and in walked the intruder. It was *her mother*.

"Mom?" Madison stopped, just barely missing colliding into Roman's back. "What are you doing here?" Complete shock filled her.

Her mother barged passed Arlo. A powerless expression was on his face. The man dealt with bad guys every day, but he'd never come face to face with an anxious mother looking for her child.

"Maddy? Darling," Connie cried out. Madison was swept into her mother's arms. The hug almost cut off her breath. "What are you doing here? I've been looking everywhere. I finally called the police. Officer Donavan kindly informed me you were here." Her fists were firmly planted on her hips. "What's going on? I want to know everything."

"I'm all right, Mom," Madison said.

Her mother narrowed her eyes at Roman. "What are you doing in this *place*?" Connie whispered in her ear.

Staring her straight in the eye, Madison held her mother at arm's length. "I think the question should be, what are you doing here?"

Her mother shot Roman another dark look. "When I heard what happened at the shop, I caught the first plane to Genoa."

"Ms. Miller," Roman said. "It's so nice to finally meet you." He held out his hand and took one of hers in both of his. "I've been looking forward to it. It's too bad that it had to happen because of such tragic circumstances." Her mother said nothing and Roman released her hand and stepped back.

Madison paused and inhaled a breath. "I'm so grateful for Roman and his family coming to my rescue. Stephanie said the shop is almost back to normal," she assured her.

"I know all I need to know about Roman and his family. My concern right now is for my daughter, not the shop."

Madison's mouth dropped open.

Eerie silence swept through the hallway. Madison was stunned by her mother's appearance at

Roman's doorstep and her attitude. What she needed now was her mother's support, not her condemnation.

Connie exhaled loudly. "My apologies, Mr. Caponelli. I've been wracked with worry ever since I heard about the attack on the shop. You can imagine my distress when I couldn't get hold of Maddy."

Thankfully, her mother had said she was sorry, but for some reason, Madison got the feeling that it was anything but sincere. Something was not right and as soon as they were alone she was damn well going to find out what that was.

"Why didn't you answer my calls?" The wrath at finding her at Roman's morphed into chastising her daughter.

Madison felt ten years old again, her mother chastising her for spending time with friends instead of getting her homework done. "I'm sorry. My phone has been sitting in rice drying out since it got wet."

Connie folded her arms across her chest and gave her the matriarchal stare, the one that said, "That's no excuse." Yes, she could have borrowed someone else's phone, but Madison had other things on her mind. The confident man who stood beside her being the main one. Well, that and trying to get things replenished for the shop. Her mother should be thanking her, not scolding her like she was a child. "Be that as it may, it's time to go. Thanks for your hospitality, Mr. Caponelli, but I can look after my daughter from here on out."

"Please call me Roman, Ms. Miller." From the

tone of his voice, she could tell he was tiring of the ungrateful exchange with her mother.

"Roman," she said between gritted teeth. Connie trapped Madison's hand in hers and hauled her toward the door.

"Mother. Stop." Madison tugged her palm free.

"It's time to go, Maddy. You shouldn't impose." Now her mother was telling her *she* was the one intruding? This was nuts.

Roman sidestepped and blocked their path. "I'm afraid that won't be possible."

Her mother gaped at him, but Madison had mixed emotions. She wasn't ready to leave, but she wouldn't stand for him, her mother, or anyone else telling her what to do.

"What do you mean by that?" Madison was almost afraid to hear the answer. They'd been getting along so well. She saw a side of Roman that hadn't elicited controlling barbarian, but was more considerate and sincere.

"We haven't finished with all the security updates that I had installed at Madison's home and the shop. There still needs to be some tests done. Not to mention Valentina is here and you two would have a chance to finish the details for your event."

"What?" Her mother stepped in front of her, her arms folded across her chest.

"The fashion show." Madison lowered her gaze, remembering the fiasco that started everything. "There were some issues with the venue we always use. Valentina offered her place, Firenza."

"Isn't that the old Costenaro place?" Connie

placed her hands on her hips. "Figures." Disgust was evident in her voice.

"Mother, you are being rude." She'd never seen her mom be so nasty to anyone before, let alone someone she was beginning to care about and one who'd offered to keep her safe.

"Yes, the old Costenaro place." Roman wasn't giving an inch and clearly didn't like her mother's insinuations regarding the past reputation of the building that once belonged to the Costenaro family, and now the Caponellis, and even if she wanted to leave with her mother, there were doubts that he would let her go. Right now, the way her mother was acting, she wouldn't go with her anyway. Something was definitely *off*.

Roman leaned his back against the entryway. It was warm for January, but they were letting a lot of cool air in, having this discussion with the door open.

"I love a place with some history. During prohibition, people gathered there to drink and gamble. Rumor has it that the feds raided it and while the cops were headed in the front, the booze and gambling tables were taken out the back and thrown in the lake." Roman's eyes sparkled devilishly as he told the story. Had he heard the stories from some of his relatives?

"I'm hoping to start an annual event based on that legend. Guests can relive the twenties. Zoot suits and flappers' dresses, pearls, and fedoras. We'll have jazz music and gambling." Valentina must have heard the conversation as she appeared out of nowhere.

"You can't have gambling," her mother argued. "It's illegal here unless on tribal land."

"It's no problem. I know a guy." He brushed it off in a teasing way. The way Roman maintained control and emanated power usually put Madison off, but right now she admired the way he stood up to her overbearing mother.

"I'm sure you do," her mother retorted.

"We might even put up a still in the back and start making our own bootlegged whiskey."

Her mother's mouth dropped open.

"Oh, Roman, you're such a jokester." Luckily, Valentina's presence seemed to calm everyone, including Madison's mother. "Hello, I'm Valentina, Roman's sister," she said to Connie. "I'm so excited to be working with Madison to make this year's fashion show the best one yet. We were just about to start on some of the details. Would you like to join us?"

Connie relaxed. "No, I'm still tired from traveling all this way. I trust Madison to do what's best for herself and the business."

"I welcome your input, Mother," Madison said. Actually, she needed her mother's support. She'd shouldered the weight of having to make all the business decisions for so long. For years it had left little time for socializing and dating. She'd resented all the responsibility at times. And with all that had taken place over the past few days, it's no wonder Madison was wound so tight.

"You've been doing just fine in my absence."

Her heart sank and Madison entwined her fingers behind her back.

"Won't you please join us for some coffee?" Valentina offered.

"No, I must be going." Connie pulled her gloves out of her pockets.

"Well, I hope we will meet up again. If you will excuse me, I'm going to start making some notes. It was very nice meeting you." With that, Valentina left, and the tension returned.

"Are you coming with me, dear? We really need to talk."

Bitterness for all the times Madison wanted to have a heart-to-heart but was ignored bubbled to the surface. "No. I'll call you later."

There was no mistaking the displeasure on her mother's face.

"All right then." Connie slipped her hands into her gloves with gusto.

"Are you certain you don't want to stay and have some coffee?" Roman played the perfect host.

"No, I've seen that Maddy is in one piece. I'm going home to rest up." Connie kissed her daughter on the cheek and ignored Roman. "I will be waiting for your call."

"Yes, Mother," she replied meekly.

"It was a pleasure, Ms. Miller. I'm sure I will be seeing you again soon," Roman said.

Madison's respect for Roman lifted a notch. Her mother was being a complete beast, but he never took the bait to engage.

"Mr. Caponelli." She nodded, choosing to ignore his request to use his first name.

"Arlo, please see Ms. Miller to her car." His comforting hand pressed against Madison's lower back to guide her back into the house. The touch sent an exhilarating chill through her along with a deep comfort.

"Sure thing, boss." Arlo closed the door behind him.

"I don't think she likes me." Roman chuckled.

"If it makes you feel any better, I wonder the same thing too." Madison fought back the tears.

Roman stopped her in her tracks on the marble entryway floor. He took her arm and without force turned her to look at him.

Madison knew her eyes were red-rimmed and glossy. The strained relationship with her mother always left a dull ache in her throat. She trapped a tear beneath her finger and tried to make light of the situation.

"You really know how to rile her. Illegal gambling…" Madison sniffled a laugh.

Roman grasped her chin in his hand and their eyes locked. Madison felt her heart flutter. He leaned down and kissed her tenderly on the lips. The pressure was light and protective but sent a slice of white lightning through her.

He pulled away, leaving only an inch between them. "I wasn't joking. I do and get what I want…But I think you already know that." Madison's breath hitched and he was right, she knew it. Roman Caponelli did and got whatever he wanted.

Chapter Twelve

Madison

Madison could walk the distance from her home to the Genoa Java Shop, but today she drove. It was hard to not still be on edge after what had happened. Armed with her favorite espresso drink, she was ready to go back to work for the first time in days. Last evening was her first night in her home after the attack. It took hours of ignoring the usual moans and groans of her home at night before she could settle down and fall asleep. She actually laughed out loud thinking back at the spectacle of Roman bursting through her bathroom door. It seemed comical now. She missed his home. It was consoling being in such a beautiful house that had everything. Madison already missed the home gym, soft bed, and luxurious bath of her guest room and the breathtaking views of the water. Scratch all of it; it was him she missed.

The fashion show as far as Firenza's part was concerned was all set and it was hard to contain her excitement about the new venue and Valentina's suggestions. Valentina was a pleasure to work with and they'd already become good friends. How nice it would have been to have her mother share in this part of the planning. Ever since she was old enough to handle things on her own, Connie had left her to do just that.

When Madison left the destruction of the shop on Saturday, she never dreamed they would be open for business again by Wednesday. Whether it was the black card, or the Caponelli name on the card, her dress orders had been shipped overnight. Normally, they could take months to arrive. The thing that took the longest was unpacking, steaming, inventorying, and re-pricing everything.

Stepping into the shop, Madison was speechless except for the *holy shit* she mumbled to herself. The place looked better than it did before. The display cabinets were all shiny and new. Apparently, Roman had a supplier in Milwaukee that special delivered them on the weekend. How they'd been able to get in when she had the key baffled her. It wasn't until Roman explained that he'd replaced all the locks both at her home and business that things finally started to settle in.

She should be furious but wasn't. It was still a little unnerving to know he also held the keys and he had a security detail watching both places on camera, but that was outweighed by her fear of that horrible man coming back. Hopefully, the guy was just some nut job passing through and the destruction was random.

The bell at the front door jingled as it opened and

jarred her back to the present. In walked her coworker and friend.

"Stephanie, I'm so glad to see you." Madison hugged her and then took a step back to get a good look at her. "How are you feeling? You look great."

"Thanks, but I know it looks bad." Steph flipped her hair to the side and Madison held back a gasp. Madison hadn't absorbed at the time how bad it really was. The damage from flying glass had cut a deep line from her cheek bone on down. It was still raw, red, and held together by stitches.

"Once the stitches are out and it's healed, I'm sure it won't be noticeable at all." Madison tried to console her friend, but the cut had been much deeper than they'd thought. When she'd last seen her it was night time, and by the light of day it appeared much worse. The wound was angry, red, and jagged.

"I hope so." Stephanie tried to shrug it off, but Madison could tell it bothered her.

"I know so." She hugged her again. "Let's get the place open and ready for business. I'm sure we'll have a lot of nosy people coming in just to find out what happened."

"I still don't know what happened," Steph said, perplexed. "Why would someone do that?" She went behind the counter to start up the computer at the register.

"Roman thinks it might be someone sending a message to him. The whole thing seems odd." She scooped up some veils that were piled on a chair. "We still need a veil rack. I've nowhere to hang these."

The front doorbell chimed again and in walked a man who nearly had to duck to cross the threshold. He had an athletic build with broad shoulders. To go along with his height, his dark hair fell well past his shoulders, and he had an alluring and sexy quality. He was simply dressed in a white shirt, black leather jacket, and jeans. Madison swallowed the lump in her throat, never taking her eyes off him as she headed straight for Stephanie and the silent alarm switch newly installed under the counter.

"May I help you?" Her voice trembled. She was grateful for the extra measures Roman had taken with their safety.

The man approached. "I have your rack." Madison blinked a few times, confused and leery.

"Um…I beg your pardon?"

The man had a slight accent but she couldn't tell from where. Her free hand still lingered below the counter, ready to push the button.

"Rack." His dark brown eyes flashed.

"Rack?" Madison tilted her head to the side.

He pointed to the tulle crowns in her arms. "From Roman. For the veils." With that, he left and both women glanced at each other.

In no time at all the guy had returned, this time carrying a heavy iron display. Just inside the door, he stopped.

Jumping out of her frightened trance, Madison pointed to where the former rack had stood. With ease, the guy carried her new display rack to the spot she indicated. The headpiece holder was like something she'd never seen before.

"This is really stunning."

It was made out of handcrafted iron. The bottom began like the roots of a tree and then rose up and split off into branches that would hold the delicate veils. The tips of the branches had crushed black velvet pads to hold the veils in place. Intricate vines and leaves accented different spots. The whole thing had been polished to a brass and black finish which matched perfectly the décor of the store.

"I've never seen anything like it." She eagerly hung a few headpieces in place. "Where did it come from?"

"I made it." A hint of a smile threatened his mouth.

"Really?" She circled the masterpiece. "And you are?"

"Dominic." The guy was not talkative, but he sure was talented.

"Do you make other things?" The craftsmanship was amazing. Her mind buzzed with ideas of other things they might need made.

"I do iron work, blacksmith stuff, and welding." At least he seemed to enjoy talking about his work. "Knives, railings, some special orders like this, but knives and swords are what I do best."

"Is there a big calling for knives and swords?" She almost hated to ask.

"In my line of work there is." His smile faded and his face was unreadable.

"Um, well. You could probably sell them or take orders. There's a community arts center in town. You could make good money from the tourists looking for a memento of Genoa."

The guy didn't say yes or no. The only thing he

seemed to take an interest in was Stephanie. Her friend may not have noticed him glancing her way, but Madison sure did.

"Stephanie has some things of her own there." She nodded to her friend behind the desk and Steph's head popped up. "You should go check it out sometime."

An awkward silence followed until Madison finally spoke. "How much do I owe you for this?"

Dominic stepped back. "Roman paid me." He turned to leave.

"Uh, are you sure?" Her debt to him was rising by the minute.

"Yes." He kept going.

"Wait," she yelled and he finally stopped. Madison stepped behind the counter and came back with a card in her hand. "This is for the Genoa Arts Center. It's for local artists. I'd really love to see more of what you can make." It was Madison's favorite place to visit. It gave her a sense of peace and she was always in awe at something she could not do like draw, paint, or carve. Madison saw the beauty in all things. Dominic glanced at the card with a twisted lip then tucked the card in his pocket and left without another word.

"Well, that was strange but I'm in love with his work." Madison placed more headpieces on the rack.

"Yeah, maybe you can go buy one of his *swords*." Hostility was edged in Stephanie's voice.

"What's wrong? Don't you like it?" Madison wondered.

"It's great, but don't you get it?" Stephanie came

around the front of the cash register. "He's not some local artisan. If he knows Roman, chances are he actually uses those knives and swords he makes on people."

Madison opened her mouth to reply at the same time a group of giggling young women strolled in the door.

She whispered, "We'll talk about this later."

It irked her that Steph had such a dislike for Roman. She could understand it, but things were different now. Madison was different. The man had been very generous and sweet. Madison was falling hard and she knew that when Stephanie realized it, their friendship was going to take a serious turn.

Chapter Thirteen

Roman

"What's wrong? Missing Madison already?" Valentina teased, pouting out her bottom lip. It was true. He'd just seen her yesterday, but it already hurt like hell. They were both in the back of one of their father's town cars—long, black, and bulletproof. Chicago was the last place he wanted to be right now and having a meeting with Rinaldi was on the top of his 'shitty stuff to deal with' list for the day.

His phone buzzed in his pocket, disturbing his thoughts. Reading it, he groaned. The message added more to the shit pile.

"That was Dom." Roman tossed his cell on the seat. "There's been an incident at the Genoa Arts Center. Similar description to the one at Madison's shop, only worse." He ran his fingers through his hair. "Guy did a lot of damage and made the same threat. This is not random and there were at least a dozen scared shitless witnesses."

"Was anyone hurt?"

"Yeah, he tossed in a small pipe bomb before he walked out the door. A few left in ambulances." Roman blew out a defeated sigh.

"What? None of this makes any sense." Valentina shook her head. "What do you think is going on?"

"I was positive it had something to do with me. But hell, I have nothing to do with the damn arts center. What the hell is going on? "

"Is it some kind of psycho who lives in town and gets off on threatening people?"

"The police said there was no one who lived there that matched the description Madison and Stephanie gave. What did you find out? Any names on your lists pop out?"

"Nothing yet, but I should be getting a printout shortly of all newly purchased properties in and around Genoa within the hour." The car slowed down as they dropped Valentina off at her hair appointment. "I'll let you know as soon as I find anything."

"Thanks, sis." He kissed her cheek.

"Have fun meeting your new fiancée."

"Don't start," he warned. Valentina exited the car and Roman slammed his fist on the seat. He dreaded the upcoming meeting. His father was already at Rinaldi's. Both men were planning his nuptials to a woman he'd never even met, while his heart was back in Genoa with the woman he wanted. He was only doing it to appease his father until he could figure out a way to tell him again this marriage was not happening.

The Rinaldi complex was similar to his father's, with high gates, lots of cameras, and security. The person at the guard shack waved them right through. His driver parked in front, and Roman left the car with a feeling of impending doom. Not in a hurry to enter, he stretched and gazed up at the fortress in front of him.

There in the window above sat a woman staring at him. Madison? He took a step. What in the world was she doing here? Instead of procrastinating, he ran up the steps two at a time. Madison was in the house. He was dumbfounded and couldn't think straight. His system flooded with fear and wonderment. It had to have been a trick of his mind. Showing up here made him realize how lovesick he was for Madison.

A maid answered the door when he rang the bell.

"Mr. Caponelli, right this way." She gestured with her hand. He followed the short woman dressed all in black.

Cigar smoke filled the air as they approached the wide expanse of the living room. Roman could hear the deep timbre of his father's voice in negotiation mode. Madison was the only thing he could concentrate on. His cell buzzed and he pulled it from his pocket. The text was from Madison.

Madison: Thank you for the beautiful display rack. Dominic is a master craftsman.

What the hell?

Roman: Where are you?

Madison: At the shop.

"Roman," his father chastised. "Don't be so rude. Put your phone away."

Roman gazed up to see Rinaldi and his father staring him down from their plush side chairs in front of an enormous fireplace. Swirls of smoke wafted up from the fat cigars they each held.

"Sorry…" he stammered. "Business." Roman shook off his bewilderment and walked to join the men in the discussion.

Roman had been up half the night coming up with alternate suggestions for bringing the families together. It was now time to tread carefully and make them.

Rinaldi stood and kissed him on both cheeks. "Welcome to my home."

"Thank you."

"Come and sit with us."

"Father." Roman nodded in acknowledgement to his dad.

Roman took a seat on the sofa across from the men.

"So," Rinaldi started. "We have been talking. Your father feels that you are apprehensive about this arranged marriage. That makes me uncomfortable." His eyebrows lowered.

Roman adjusted in his seat. His father offered no interference or support.

"Sir, I mean no disrespect. But I feel that we can make some other new arrangement. I hold your family and honor in the highest regard." It was true. Roman had no reason to dislike or grudge Rinaldi's family. If his father thought it was a good alliance, then he couldn't argue. He would go with his gut.

"Going against the family's wishes is not keeping the family number one." Rinaldi had a point.

"Blood oaths have been an accepted practice among united families all the way back to Italy," Roman countered.

Rinaldi's face puffed and reddened. "Is my daughter not good enough for you?"

"Sir, I mean no disrespect. I am simply offering another solution." Roman had never even met his daughter.

His father's eyes narrowed at him. This was a blatant act of defiance against the family. His father could strip him of his title and disown him. He could wage bloody war against Roman if he wanted to. But his father was getting up in age and his taste for the *life* had grown tiresome. Roman marrying Rinaldi's daughter was his retirement plan. A smart one set in motion years ago but not one Roman was willing to forfeit his happiness for. Not to mention the fact that he'd killed Diego, one of Rinaldi's men. No one but Madison and the men who were there really knew the truth of what happened. Nevertheless, he had to stall this.

"Sir, I thank you for your hospitality but I regret to inform you that I cannot possibly marry your daughter."

Rinaldi sat forward in his seat, steam coming out of his ears.

Roman's father yelled, "What?"

"I cannot marry her, Father. I am already

engaged."

Chapter Fourteen

Madison

"Are you even listening to me?" Her mother's voice jarred her from her thoughts.

Roman had left on Wednesday and it was hard to concentrate on anything else. He was all she could think about and usually that would anger her, but lately she'd become more contented with the idea of having him around. It was becoming second nature.

When they first met last year at the ball, she knew he was *Mr. Right*. Finding out he dabbled on the wrong side of the law dashed her hopes but it was the heart, not the head that began to rule her. Try as she might to fight it, she cared for him a lot. How much she cared was yet to be seen. Her mother and Stephanie were not fans, but in time he would win them both over or they would have to learn to live with it.

Despite their opposite upbringing, they had a lot of things in common. Roman's reasons for coming to Genoa being a very important one. He admitted at their dinner that he'd come to the small town to get away from it all and settle down. They both wanted to have a family and raise their children where they knew all their neighbors and could be very involved in the community. His plans for Firenza were just a small part of what he had planned for diversifying his families dealings into more legitimate businesses.

Roman had asked her thoughts on many of his ideas. One that she was particularly excited about was a winery. After her suggestion, he looked into it and found one that he was interested in purchasing. With over one hundred wineries in Wisconsin, the state was becoming a major player in the wine world. Roman had family in Italy that ran a vineyard and they'd be an important asset to that venture.

She had fallen under his spell. Just the sound of his voice triggered her heart to beat faster. Thinking of his eyes staring into hers caused her to swoon. Dreaming about waking up with him in the morning affected her like no man ever had. Thoughts that he'd killed men sent a chill down her spine and created a pit of nausea in her stomach. He may be a dangerous man, but she knew in her soul that he would die to protect her. Her heart may say yes, but her head still wasn't sure that getting involved with the Caponellis was the right thing to do.

"Madison?" Connie had put down her fork and raised her eyebrows. "Are you listening to me?"

"I'm sorry. What were you saying?" Madison chased a strawberry around her plate with her fork at one of the finest historic homes in Genoa that also happened to be a restaurant. Sunday champagne brunch was her favorite but this morning she had no appetite and it was due to the fact that she missed Roman.

The whole town was on edge after the incident at her shop and worse yet, the arts center. It was by chance that Dominic had stopped by the place. He'd just parked his truck and was about to go in when he spied the bad guy running out of the building. It was just seconds later that the glass was blown out of the windows.

Nothing about him being a witness was in the news, but when Roman had phoned earlier he mentioned that Dom had been there. It was the same man who'd been at Bells and Bows. Dominic had described him in great detail. With both the police and Roman on the lookout for the creep, chances were good he'd be brought to justice, but for the town's sake, it wasn't soon enough.

"I was talking about the music for the show." Connie took a sip of her champagne, her pinky finger straight out.

"Oh yes, I tend to try to stick with classical, but seeing that it will be at Firenza maybe we should add in some Italian love songs as well."

Her mother eyed her suspiciously. "What is it, Maddy? I know something is wrong."

"I'm worried," she blurted out.

"The show will be fine. It always is."

How would she know? Connie was rarely there. "It's not that." Madison sighed and set her fork on the table. "I'm worried about Roman and what's going on in town. He thinks the threats might be a warning to him. Someone could have been killed at the arts center." She took a sip of water. "Can you image if it'd been Stephanie's day to volunteer there after what happened at the shop? She'd probably never leave her house again."

"If you want my opinion…" Connie leaned in closer. "I think you should put Roman right out of your mind." Her mother tapped her temple. "He's probably the one behind all this, or some other awful mafia trash trying to move in."

"That's not fair. You don't even know him." Madison picked up her utensils and began cutting her French toast into pieces with a vengeance.

"I know more than you think of his kind." Her mother sipped from her champagne glass again and eyed Madison.

"Oh, really, Mother, and what exactly is *his kind*?"

Again, Connie took another healthy swig of her champagne and set the crystal flute on the table. "He's very handsome and *experienced*." She paused, choosing her words. "He sees a small town girl as an easy mark. I've heard all about his reputation with the ladies." Connie seemed to be waiting for a response, but instead interjected. "Romeo, I believe they call him in the papers." Her mother widened her eyes and folded her arms across her chest. "Why can't you find a nice local boy to settle down with? What about that nice police officer, Ryan something or other?"

"Roman is nothing like he's portrayed in the papers." Madison stared her mother straight in the eye. "I grew up with all the local boys, remember?

Not one of them is Roman." Madison popped a large piece of toast in her mouth and chewed, annoyed beyond belief. "You're not even giving him a chance."

She reached out and placed her hand on top of Madison's. "I don't want you to make the same mistakes that I, uh…that others have made."

As much as she wanted to ask more, Madison kept her mouth shut. She didn't have the tolerance today to have a deep, heavy discussion with her mother. There was enough on her mind.

Her phone buzzed and the sound made her leap, yanking her from her thoughts.

Roman: On my way back.

Madison exhaled and relaxed in her chair.

Roman: Can I see you today?

"Speak of the devil," her mother huffed, and Madison frowned. Connie didn't need to see the screen on her phone to know who was texting her.

"I don't understand you. Roman and Valentina are nice. Look at all they did to help with the shop."

Madison: Yes. Call me when you get back.

"She seemed like a smart young woman but…" Connie trailed off while Madison laid her phone back on the crowded table.

"No more buts." She finished her drink in one gulp. "I have feelings for this man. Please respect that my life is my life, not yours." Madison held a finger up to her mother.

Her mother took the napkin from her lap and tossed it on the table. "All right, but know this. If he ever hurts you, don't say I didn't warn you. If you need me, I will always be here."

Madison was speechless. It was on the tip of her tongue to ask what made this any different than any other situation that might arise in which she might need her mother, but she remained quiet.

"Okay, fine."

The waiter arrived with some coffee and Madison stirred in two teaspoons of sugar. Her spoon rattled on the side of the China cup as she stirred.

"So, why don't we go over the lineup for the fashion show again?" Madison was eager to change the subject.

A busboy arrived to clear their plates and Madison got out her pen and paper. She'd left her tablet at home, not knowing if they would really be working on the show or not.

"I'm sorry," her mother whispered, but she heard her clear as day.

"For what?"

"I have…" Connie choked up. "I only wanted to do the right thing."

"Of course, Mother. I love you." This had turned into the strangest brunch.

Her mother just smiled. "Just remember what I said."

Madison was pleased the conversation transitioned to the show. She and her mother ended up enjoying a steaming cup of tea in the salon later, and working on the show for another couple of hours.

Her mother appeared to relax and even enjoy collaborating, something that she usually left all on Madison's lap.

"Thanks, Mom."

"For what?" Connie lifted her shoulders.

"I can't tell you how much I've enjoyed working on this together with you."

"It's time for me to step up to the plate. You've worked so hard all these years and that's one of the reasons that I've returned for good."

Madison almost choked on her tea. "For good?"

"Yes, it's been selfish of me to be traveling all over the world while you shouldered the burdens of running Bells and Bows. It's time that *you* follow *your* dreams."

Madison was stunned. This was so out of left field.

"What do you mean?" She'd been waiting to hear this for years, but it was the last thing she expected to happen.

"You're so talented. You could be a designer like you always dreamed about."

Madison crossed her legs, intrigued.

"Well, I had considered putting one of the dresses I created in the show, but with everything going on, it's been the last thing on my mind."

"Don't worry about that. I'm back and it's time for you to focus on your career."

"Career?" Madison swallowed.

"Yes. I just returned from New York." Connie

leaned over and snatched a petit four from the plate of goodies on the tray in front of them. "I ran into Fran, an old college friend of mine. You'll never believe this, but she runs a design house there. They specialize in bridal and formal couture."

Madison's pulse raced, both hoping and dreading what her mother would say next.

"I showed her some pictures of the designs you've done and she's offered you an internship with her company. Isn't it exciting? You can finally follow your dream." Connie hugged her tight before letting go and popping the treat in her mouth.

"I don't know what to say." She was in shock. It was everything Madison had ever dreamed about since she could remember. Well, until recently that was. Her head spun. "Why didn't you mention this before?"

"I wanted it to be a surprise and with everything going on, it just didn't seem like the right time." Her mother reached into her purse and pulled out her phone. "So when should I let Fran know you'll be coming?"

Madison's phone buzzed. It was Roman. "I…" She stared down at her phone.

Roman: I'm back. Can you come over? Or I could meet you at your place? I have a meeting but I'll be done soon.

"Don't worry about the show. I will handle everything," Connie said.

"I don't know. It's all so sudden." A mismatch of thoughts bounced in her head. It was the chance of a lifetime. It had been her dream since she was a little girl.

"It's about time. You're not getting any younger. Life is short, don't let what you want pass you by." Her mother's finger slid across her phone's screen. Madison took a deep breath and reached for her mother's hand. "Umm…Thank you. You have no idea how much I appreciate this opportunity."

***

Madison closed her eyes and enjoyed the luxury of heated seats as Arlo drove her to Roman's home. He had a business meeting to finish up in town before they met so Arlo picked her up from her home. A girl could get used to being driven around. She hated driving when the roads were slippery and today the roads were a little slick with the remnants of a short snowfall last night.

The whole day, she'd felt like she was skating on thin ice. So many things had happened in such a short time. Their time apart had been tough, but it'd given her time to think. Her goal ever since she'd been a little girl had been to design dresses. Her mother's offer of the internship with her friend's design company was impossible to resist. Her designs could be in the shop windows next to the likes of Vera Wang, Marchesa, and Carolina Herrera.

Numbly, she waved to the guard who stood at the gatehouse. Madison bit her lip and entwined her fingers on her lap.

"Are you warm enough?" Arlo asked.

"Yes, I'm fine."

"You've been quiet today." He never missed anything.

"I spent the day with my mother planning the fashion show. I think I'm talked out."

"How's that going?" Arlo pulled the car up in front of the house and put it in park.

"Good. I think we are all set, but you know how things go. Just when you think you have everything figured out, someone throws a wrench into the picture."

He chuckled. "Isn't that the truth?"

They'd barely parked and she was out of the car and in the door. Her heart was in her throat. She had to tell him before she lost her nerve.

"Madison," he called from above.

Roman was just coming down the stairs, a dazzling smile on his face. Gone was the suit and tie, this time replaced by blue jeans, an ivory sweater, and heavy plaid shirt. He looked every bit the local guy.

As soon as his feet touched the bottom stair, she rushed over and Roman engulfed her in his arms. His familiar scent was both welcoming and intoxicating. The internship offer was like a pit in her stomach as she soaked up Roman's warmth.

"So to what do I owe this wonderful greeting?" His smile made her knees weak.

"We need to talk." Her eyes watered.

Chapter Fifteen

Roman

It was so good to be home. Amazing how fast the area had become a sanctuary to him. His refuge from fighting over territories, busting bones, and his father's insistence that he marry someone he didn't love. He now held the one he wanted in his arms.

Roman wanted way more than he took. He wanted to scoop Madison up into his arms and race with her to his bedroom to keep her to himself. Instead, his instincts told him not to. She wasn't there…yet. He would have her, though. His father and his ancient marriage views be damned. Madison was what he wanted in a wife and she would be his. The man was getting old. Not that Roman didn't respect his father, but times had changed. There were other ways to unite their families. He didn't have to marry Rinaldi's daughter to do it.

Grabbing her hand in his, they headed to his office. "You're trembling."

"I'm just a little cold."

He shut the door behind her. "I can help you with that," he said, wiggling his eyebrows.

Madison held up her hand like she was stopping traffic. "I have something to say before I lose my nerve."

Roman leaned against his desk. This wasn't good, and his jaw twitched at what could possibly be making her like this. He'd fought to the death a couple times but never felt so helpless.

"Go on," he urged.

Madison paced and wrung her hands. "Today, my mother made me an offer that was too good to refuse."

She stopped and briefly glanced out the window before returning to the track she was marking on the rug. "It's always been a goal of mine since I was a kid to be a designer."

"I know that and I would never do anything to stop you from reaching your ambitions."

"I was offered a position at a couture house in New York."

A pit settled in his stomach. It was hard enough to spend the time he wanted in Genoa until he could finagle his work more to this area. He tightened his grip on the edge of the desk. His fist was clenched so tight on the frame of the desk he thought it might snap.

"And?" He needed to hear it was over before deciding on his plan. She was his, there had to be a way to work it out. Madison deserved everything but he'd never let her go so far away.

"And I realized that it was exactly that, my goal as a kid. Thirty is creeping up on me. What I want in life has changed." Roman raised his gaze from the floor to meet her eyes. His heart thumped in agony of what she was going to say.

"What I want in life is you." Madison stood across the room, but he heard her loud and clear.

Roman swore his heart skipped a beat or two in the last few seconds. Now it was likely to jump from his chest. She said she wanted him but the smug alpha male in him wanted more. He was going to make her prove it.

"Then come get me," he demanded as his breathing picked up.

His woman marched across the room. Her cheeks flushed and her eyes were wild.

Her hands framed his face, fingers trembling slightly. Her lips neared his and when they touched, he was lifted to heaven. She tasted sweet, like the chocolate cake she loved. When Madison slipped her tongue between his lips, he nearly burst at the seams.

Pulling her into his arms, he swung her around and onto the desk. Her legs wrapped around his waist, right where they belonged. Roman deepened the kiss, determined to forever brand it into her mind. He touched and took whatever he wanted and she let him. His sweater hit the floor and she roamed her free hands over his chest. He squeezed her shoulders before tearing her blouse, revealing a white bra with tiny crystals and lace reminding him of a bridal gown. The sight of it fed his passion. Madison reached out and unclasped his jeans, freeing him without breaking the kiss. She slid them down his thighs. Her fingers raked over his thick shaft. Roman thought he would explode. He dipped his hands into the back of her pants, squeezing until she squealed. There was no stopping him. He would take her then and there.

This sealed the deal. Madison was his and he was never letting go.

Madison

She declared her goals in life and in him, and it was amazing. However, he'd never confessed his feelings for her. Last night was overwhelming and now she was suddenly shy. Roman had carried her to his room naked and made love to her again. A few times during the night, she'd awakened, not used to being wrapped in someone's arms. His muscle bound arm held her tight to his chest. A long, hair roughened leg had been wrapped possessively around one of hers. Just the thought of being together again sent heat searing through her veins. It was definitely something she could get used to.

Madison stood and stretched, alone in the room. A few pops and kinks relieved the tension. Spying her purse on the table, she made a grab for it, only to stub her toe loudly on the table leg.

"I'll have coffee ready in a sec." Roman popped his head around the door. He walked over and kissed her on the cheek. His warm arms wrapped reassuringly around her waist. Sometime during the night, she'd lost all her clothes and was traveling around only in her socks. There was no quick getaway now. No boots, no car, and he'd already seen she was up.

She might as well make the best of it, eat some breakfast and go home.

She bared her heart.

They made love.

Was that all he'd been after? Was she just another chapter in his little black book?

She should have ducked when he kissed her cheek, but it was too late. Her flesh tingled from the graze of his lips.

"I'd love to take you back to bed." He moaned the words. "But I have another meeting today." Kissing the top of her shoulder, he hugged her once more. "I'll meet you in the kitchen when you're ready." With another quick kiss, he was gone.

Fumbling with the light switch in the bathroom, she avoided the mirror for as long as possible. Her lips were swollen and her hair was a mess. Taking a quick shower, Madison washed her hands and face and did a little touch up with whatever makeup she could find in her bag. Fortunately, there was also a comb and a headband to tame the mangled mess her hair had become. She gave her refection a half smile, took a deep breath, and set off to say a quick farewell to Roman.

He hadn't kicked her out, but instead asked her to breakfast. Maybe she was just overreacting. Some guys just weren't good about sharing their feelings. She'd survive and move on. Putting a brave face on, she wandered to the kitchen, prepared to put him and his incredible lovemaking skills out of her mind. If she had become another notch on the bedpost, she'd have to live with that.

Easier said than done. Who could resist a handsome man in the kitchen stirring some eggs around in a pan? His dark hair was ruffled from sleep, and there was a white dish towel thrown over his shoulder. Sometime during the night, he'd changed into a pair of flannel pants and a long-sleeved Henley. The urge to wrap her arms around him from behind and rest her cheek on his shoulder raced out from somewhere. He looked nothing like the deadly gangster she tried to convince herself he was.

"Have a sit." Taking the warm mug he handed her, she added some sugar and creamer that was on the counter, and strolled to the table they'd had dinner at recently. Although it was cozy in the house, she automatically gripped each side of the cup to warm her fingers. This morning, the view of the lake was breathtaking. A few early risers were walking their dogs. She chuckled at the guy who had a leash in one hand and a filled convenience bag of poop in the other.

"I hope you like scrambled. That's the extent of my egg making skills."

Her stomach growled. Except for a midnight raid on the refrigerator for some cannoli and hot cocoa, they'd not had a bite to eat. It was on the tip or her tongue to say no, but as soon as the plate was in front of her, she dug in with gusto.

"Thank you. I…" Madison took a bite of toast and then a forkful of eggs. Her taste buds sang. This guy was either the world's best egg maker or she was starving to death. He was obviously a better cook than he admitted.

136

Everything he did seemed to surprise her as normal, comforting, and Roman pulled her closer. Madison was afraid that her heart would be crushed beyond repair.

There was nothing normal or comforting about him. He caused her heart to race, her stomach to flutter, and her arms naturally wanted to pull him near.

"Is something wrong?" He had been watching her over his cup of coffee but now he placed it on the table. "You're so quiet." Roman talked while he buttered his toast. She had a hard time deciding where to look, at his face or at his tanned hands as they scraped a knife across the bread.

Okay, she seriously had to leave if watching him put butter on bread left her lightheaded. "I really should be going." She started to rise but the light pressure of his hand on hers sat her back down.

"No." The expression on his face screamed she wasn't going anywhere. "Tell me what's wrong. I want to know now."

"I want to leave with at least a bit of dignity."

"What? Why?" His eyes were huge.

"Isn't this how it goes with you? A one-nighter, then the woman is driven home. Should I call for Arlo or will you? "

"Why the hell do you think I don't want to see you anymore?" Roman appeared angry.

"Well, it's just that I told you how deeply I felt for you last night, but you never said a word about how you felt about me. I guess I should call you Romeo now."

He stood up so fast his chair fell backward and

Madison jumped.

"Don't ever doubt me." In the next moment, he was on his knee in front of her. "I've never kneeled before anyone, but I am for you. From the first moment I laid eyes on you, I knew you were meant for me. I'm sorry I didn't say how I felt last night, but I was overwhelmed. Stunned that the one I wanted for so long was finally mine."

Madison was speechless.

"Do you understand me?" His fingers caressed her cheek and she nodded. Roman reinforced the words with a passionate kiss. Standing, he picked up the chair and sat next to her. "Never doubt my feelings for you. In fact, I want you to meet my parents. Soon."

"What?" Her jaw dropped. His confession kick-started her heart, but the thought of meeting his parents scared her to death.

"Don't worry, they will love you. We will go after your show."

"Uh, okay." Madison chewed her toast and processed all that he had said. Her thoughts were a jumbled mess. He'd said she was meant for him, but he still hadn't said anything about love. It was a start. Still, she felt a little awkward. "Well, I'd better go so you can get to your meeting."

"No you don't. What do you have to do today?" His eyes locked onto hers.

"Nothing." It was the first thing that popped into her mind. What did she do on Sundays? Not much.

"Perfect."

"What do you mean?" Madison started to eat again. She really was ravenous.

"Then we can spend the day together."

"I really don't think that's a good idea." Her mind struggled to come up with reasons why it wasn't. "I need to process everything that has happened."

"Afraid you might seduce me back into bed?" Roman smirked and raised one eyebrow.

"No." This time she couldn't meet his eyes.

"Too bad." He lifted her hand to kiss it. "I was hoping that would happen, but since you have nothing planned and you're no longer concerned about how I feel about you, what do you say we go on a drive together?"

"Yes." Taking a sip of coffee, the temperate liquid heated her throat the whole way down. Their relationship would be like no other and yet she could not walk away.

"I have to drive to Milwaukee. I thought we could do lunch, see some sites." He grabbed a nearby newspaper. "Spend time together."

She nodded and glanced out the window again. It was useless to argue a case she didn't want to win. "That sounds nice." They ate in comfortable silence. For some reason, Madison never felt the need to fill in the quiet time with words. She was content just being around him. Maybe he did care as much as he said.

Roman handed her the paper while he gathered their plates. "Take your time. I'm going to set these in the kitchen, call Arlo, and then we will be on our way."

"Wait."

"Yes?"

"Could we stop by my place for a few minutes? I'd like to change clothes."

"Of course."

Roman left the room. Instead of reading the news, she took a moment to soak in her surroundings. Sunny mornings, drinking coffee and reading papers together was a start.

Madison had to keep her head. She needed to come to terms with the unsavory side of Roman's work. Things were moving way too fast.

A relationship, or even marriage, was for better or worse. Last night, she'd only thought of the good things. If she was really going to be with Roman, and that's what she wanted, it was time to face the reality of what she was getting into. In life, a person didn't pick who they fell for. She'd fallen hard for Roman. If she was going to live in his world, she had to know everything, whether it was the good, bad, or nasty.

"Ready to go?" His smile always lit up the room.

"Yes." Madison may have had determination to take things slowly, but it was going to be a hard battle to win.

Chapter Sixteen

Madison

It felt heavenly to wash her hair and have a new set of clothes on. Roman spoke in Italian the whole time he talked to Arlo on the phone. At least, that's who she thought he was talking to. After helping her into her coat, she buckled up and they were on the road to Milwaukee. It was only about a forty-five minute drive from Genoa.

"Where's Arlo?"

Roman checked the rear and side windows before backing out into the street. "He's in town already."

"Really? When he dropped me off last night, I got the impression that he was staying to take me home."

"Well, that didn't happen, did it?" He turned and winked. "And something came up in Brew Town, so I sent him ahead."

"Is it business?" She feared it was the kind of business she didn't want to hear about.

"Yes, it's a fire at one of our warehouses." He briefly squeezed her hand before returning his attention to the shifter. "Nothing to worry about."

Madison stared ahead and tried to calm the feelings of foreboding. She was determined to deal with whatever came from being with him and she'd enjoy every moment. The miles flew by. Roman really was an interesting person. She'd learned more about him in the hours that she'd spent in the vehicle than she knew about others she'd known for a lifetime. They had reconnected quickly, like they did at the Snowflake Ball. It seemed natural to be in each other's company, but her heart wanted to know everything.

He'd briefly touched on what it was like to grow up in a mafia family. He touched on the coldness he felt between himself and his father.

"I admired my father and I knew that how he treated me was for my own good and the good of the family. I didn't have an option of what I wanted to be when I grew up. I came to terms with that very quickly." Roman sighed and seemed thoughtful. "You can't choose your family or the one you fall in love with." Madison's heart jumped in her chest at his words. She couldn't argue with that. She'd never seen eye to eye with her mother.

Roman mentioned that he had attended college and earned a business degree. He had aspirations of moving *the family* to more and more legal businesses. That alone made her hopeful that things would work out between them. They'd stopped at a burger place for lunch and it was so normal and natural to be with him. It was a comfort she hadn't

142

ever felt before.

"I have to make a stop," Roman announced. He drove them to a different part of town and Madison could tell something wasn't right. There were way too many black sedans and SUVs, the kind that Roman always used. Arlo and another man stood by one of the vehicles and they did not look pleased.

Roman parked nearby, but told her to wait in the car. Too curious for her own good, she lowered the window to hear.

Madison watched as Roman greeted each person with a nod and a handshake. They all held themselves in the same manner and were clearly of Italian decent. The air held a razor sharp edge to it as if a bomb could explode at any moment set off by testosterone.

"Fenetti, what happened here?" Fortunately, they spoke English.

"What I told you would happen. They want to take over and they want revenge for what happened to Diego."

Roman cursed and ran his fingers through his hair. His face went from lighthearted, like it had been with her, to stone cold.

"I say we strike and we strike now," the man they addressed as Fenetti demanded. "Either you do…or I will."

Madison

After pushing every button that the door had until the window closed, Madison tried to ignore the conversation going on nearby. She wasn't stupid.

They meant *business*. Whoever started the blaze would pay. How they compensated, she wasn't sure and didn't want to know. She was already so taken with Roman that she'd turn a blind eye to whatever he did. She'd already done it once. Resting her elbow on the armrest, she glanced at the group again.

Roman and Fenetti were animated to say the least. Both up in each other's faces, arms waving in the air. Even with the window closed, she could hear some of what they said. Arlo, always the quiet soldier, took turns observing the two in front of him and their surroundings. Finally, everyone quieted and it seemed like they'd reached some kind of an agreement.

Ever so slightly, she observed Arlo lean closer to hear. Fenetti smiled and embraced Roman in a big hug. They shook hands and the taller of the two motioned in her direction with a sexy grin. Her cheeks flushed. Had she been caught eavesdropping? All three men approached the vehicle she was in.

Struggling with the damn buttons again, Roman opened the door before she could find the right one.

"Madison. I'd like to introduce you to someone." The man next to him took off his hat and held it in both hands in front of him. "This is Oscar Fenetti. He runs the territory here."

Meekly, she held out her hand to shake. "It's a pleasure, Mr. Fenetti."

"Ah, the bridal shop owner. Please call me Oscar." He seemed genuinely pleased to meet her. "Welcome to the family."

The family? She nodded. Roman winked at her and with an arm around his shoulder, he led Fenetti back to where they had been talking. With a hug and more hand and arm shakes, they went their separate ways. Arlo stayed with Fenetti, and Roman returned to her side.

"Sorry about the delay. We had to sort a few things out." He leaned against the open door looking more handsome than should be legal. Even though it was Sunday and she was in jeans, he was dressed as if heading for the office—his long legs encased in dark khaki pants, wide shoulders filling out a turquoise patterned sweater, the brown leather jacket making his sable hair even darker. Her fingers itched and she reached out and caressed his five o'clock shadow. The black whiskers gave him a devilish appearance that she couldn't resist.

Maybe she was the one with dark side, the urge to go after things that were bad for her. Stuff like sinful chocolate, impossible dreams, and mafia men.

"Is everything all right?" Roman took her hand.

"Yes, why?" A lot of things weren't right, but try as she may, there was no saying no to him.

"You had the strangest look on your face. Are you sure you're okay?"

"Yes, I'm shocked at how bad the fire was." She gave herself an imaginary pat on the back for coming up with a quick answer and her eyes turned to rest briefly on the charred building. There was no reason except confusion for the mixture of emotions flowing through her body.

Roman turned to look at the building that had

once been one of his warehouses. The smoldering embers still glowed in the ashes.

"What was in the buildings?"

"Inventory." He let go of her hand, shut the door, and hurried to the other side.

The piney scent of his cologne reassured her as he settled his weight into the seat.

"At least you have insurance," she said.

"Don't worry. We'll be *compensated* for it." The edge to his voice sent a chill down her spine. He reached for her hand again and the wariness disappeared. "Do you want to eat somewhere here before we go?"

"No, I'd rather go back to Genoa." Madison had never been a big city girl. She couldn't wait to return home. "Do you like Chinese food?"

"Love it. Is there a place you'd like to go there?"

"Yes, it's a little place next to the Genoa Arts Center."

"The place that was bombed? I had Arlo check out the damage but I've yet to get there."

"It's along the lake on the west side." The heated seat warmed her behind.

"I've heard of that area. It's one of the few spots that aren't heavily developed."

"Yes, it's really old. The arts center is in an old barn and the restaurant is a remodeled auto shop."

"What other things do they do at the arts center besides sell stuff? Plays and concerts?" Roman expertly weaved their way through traffic and they were soon on the highway.

"No, it's just for craft items, books, canned goods." She waved her free hand in the air as she talked. "Anything that's made by a local resident."

"So do you have any of your designer dresses there?" He knew of her passion for designing gowns, a passion that had been fading away with time.

"No, but Stephanie has some of her writings there."

Roman glanced over with a raised eyebrow. "A writer, huh? Have you read some of her stuff?"

"Yes. It's really good and she's working on some mystery and suspense novels now."

"It's no mystery that she doesn't like me," Roman joked.

Madison puffed her lower lip out. She shrugged and made a mental note to ask her about that on Monday.

"Yeah." She squeezed his hand that was still holding hers. "Anyway, she's an aspiring writer and she's got a few short stories that she published under a pen name there."

"Interesting."

"Are you a reader?"

"Sometimes."

"Really?"

"Yes. I'll have to check out the place."

"I told Dominic that he should put some things there. The rack he made was amazing. I can't wait to see the other things he makes." They didn't have any merchandise like that at the store.

"He can do anything. He's actually making some iron flower boxes and railings for Firenza. He also does swords, candle holders, and stuff like that."

"Wow, as far as I know they don't carry iron

items, so that would be a great addition." She would make a point to have Stephanie let her know if he showed up there. "Have him stop by the shop and they will get him set up. They pay by commission and the crafter has to help at the shop a couple days a month."

Roman cringed. "I'll tell him you're interested in him being there, but he's not real social. I'm positive he won't want to work with customers." He entwined his fingers with hers and she resisted the urge to pull him closer. "Maybe they can work something out. He's very handy, just not..." He seemed to search for the right word. "He's not good with people."

"That can be said for a lot of folks these days. I swear if Stephanie didn't work at the shop, she'd never get out. Her favorite thing is to stay home and read a book or do some writing."

"Are you warm enough?" Roman had shed his coat before getting in the vehicle but she'd kept hers on.

"Yes, I am loving these heated seats." Crossing her leg over the other, it was easy to imagine spending lazy weekends together. After struggling with the decision of whether or not to date a mafia man for months, it didn't seem to matter during moments like this.

"If you get cold, let me know and I'll crank up the heat."

"I'm sure you're very good at that." She couldn't help but tease, and he drew her hand over and dropped a kiss on the back of it.

"You have no idea."

Laughter followed as they bantered back and forth. Reluctantly, she let go of his hand as they reached heavier traffic.

Folding her arms across her chest, she studied his profile. Pieces of his dark hair had fallen across his forehead and she yearned to feel the roughness of his whiskers along her neck. Madison slipped off her coat.

"I told you I could crank up the heat and I didn't even have to hit the button," he joked.

"Ha, ha." It was hard to deny the effect he had on her. "This friend of yours, Dominic. The one that isn't, as you say, very social."

"You seem very interested in him. Are you trying to make me jealous?"

"Would you be?"

"Of course."

"I was just thinking maybe he might be someone who would get along with Stephanie. You know, since they both seem to have something in common."

"Oh yeah, how so?"

"Well, you know." For some reason, he didn't seem too excited about fixing up a friend of his with a friend of hers. "Because they seem to be so similar. Both are artistic, loners. They might hit it off."

"I don't know about that," he grumbled.

"I think they'd be great."

"Who?"

"You know who. The blacksmith." She relaxed into the seat as they moved away from the heavy traffic of the big city.

"Dominic?" Roman exhaled loudly. "He's had a troubled past. I'm not sure he's relationship material."

"Well, you know, to some woman that's a challenge."

"A relationship should never be a challenge."

"Yes, that's true." She frowned. "Yet, you want to date me even though we have our differences."

He reached for her hand again. The warmth from his fingers flowed up her arms and caused her heart rate to quicken.

"We have outside issues. That's something that we can overcome. Dominic has internal issues. Some things can't be fixed."

"Love can mend anything." She'd always believed in that. Love could conquer all, as they say.

"You really mean that?" A slight smile graced his lips.

"Yes, I do." Madison straightened her spine.

"So does that mean that you'll go to Chicago and meet my parents?" He turned and gave her a grin that was both playful and sexy as sin.

Her heart yelled "yes," but her mind urged caution. Roman was the kind of man who did nothing halfway. It was important that she keep her independence and not be swept away.

"I will, but…" She paused. "On one condition."

"I don't like stipulations."

"I think you will be able to handle this one."

"Okay. What is it?"

"No more of the mob tactics. You forced my hand into having my show at your sister's place. I won't be forced into doing anything like that again."

"That was business."

"That resulted in me going on a date."

"Sorry, but I'm a bastard sometimes." He winked at her again, being so playful.

"You didn't give me a choice."

"I'm used to making decisions for the betterment of the family, so I went a little overboard knowing that arrangement would benefit both of us." He looked her straight in the eye. "I promise not to do that again."

"Then yes, I would love to meet them." He smiled, tugged her hand over, and rested it on his thigh. "Don't let it happen again."

"It won't happen again. You have my word."

Chapter Seventeen

Roman

Roman took a glance at his watch for the tenth time in an hour. He had a surprise for Madison and was counting off the minutes until he could show her. Impatiently, he finished the last bit of his work for the morning and pushed his chair away from the desk. The view from the window drew him closer. It wouldn't be long before the tranquil lake would be filled with energetic tourists and locals boating, swimming, and fishing. The winter had been a mild one. Even now, the ice threatened to edge away from the shoreline.

Today he had to go back to the windy city. The pressure was on from the family and he could only be gone for so long. A meeting with Rinaldi was on the schedule for the evening. Roman clenched his fist and leaned a shoulder against the cool window. If he ever needed a poker face, now would be the time. Lying never came easy for him. Yes, he could bluff and con his way out of things with the best of them, but in this case, he'd have to look the guy straight in the eye and convince him that it wasn't his gun that had killed one of his men. Most importantly, he had to put a stop to this contract marriage.

His father didn't care that he was already engaged. It was a lie, but one he intended to correct soon. The ring he had for Madison wasn't an engagement ring, but to anyone looking at it from a distance it would appear so. It was too early to ask her to marry him. Damn, he wanted to, but she deserved a proper proposal and with everything going on, the time just wasn't right.

He popped open the small black velvet box. It held a stunning blue sapphire that matched the color of her eyes and the band had small diamonds around it. The sooner it was on her finger, the better. Roman planned to stop by her store and give it to her before leaving town. Madison would probably say it was too much, but in this case he wasn't taking no for an answer. As far as his woman was concerned, he never would.

Roman put on his coat, tucked the box in his pocket, and slipped his overnight bag over his shoulder.

"Arlo, get the car. I'm ready to go." He spoke into his cell and walked out the door.

Madison

Madison hummed and it wasn't just because of the coffee cup in her hand. No, her time with Roman had her floating on air. Thinking of him made her morning stroll to the Java Shop even more enjoyable. Most of the lakeshore—the centerpiece of the town—was lined with homes, mansions, resorts, and restaurants. The first twenty feet of the shoreline had been declared public domain many years ago by early settlers. A paved path completely surrounded the lake for people to walk and enjoy the view.

All of it was beautiful, but the part of town she hiked through today was one of her favorites. The mostly undeveloped site and the surrounding buildings had been there for over a hundred years. They could probably list it as a historical district, but no one had bothered to go through the paperwork. Roman had joked about it being an excellent place to upgrade. Lake Genoa was perfect the way it was and she never wanted it to change.

They'd spent the past couple weeks getting to know each other, both mentally and physically. He'd become her addiction. The more they were together, the more she wanted him. After the fashion show, he was taking her to Chicago to meet his parents. Butterflies attacked her stomach every time she thought about it. The idea of meeting his father terrified her.

The sun's rays heated her face. Madison stopped at the corner, closed her eyes and lifted her chin to the sky. Even though it was February, the sun felt warm. She wanted to soak in every drop. Today was above freezing. It was amazing how forty degrees in the springtime felt balmy while the same temperature in October was unbearable. Every winter, neighbors complained about the cold, yet no one wanted to move away. They might take a week's trip to Florida or somewhere more temperate, but everyone always returned.

Yearning for the first hints of spring, she opened her eyes and headed for work. The sidewalks were now ice free and the barren yards showed more ground than snow. It wouldn't be long. She glanced to the trees in the hopes a robin might be there but that was wishful thinking. The tips of her fingers hugged the insulated cup to stay warm. She'd abandoned her warm gloves for fingerless ones. It was hard not to be giddy knowing there were more sunny days ahead. Winter took its toll on everyone.

"Morning." She greeted an older couple out walking their poodles. They nodded and the canines wagged their tails.

The storefront of Bells and Bows came into view. It was a love-hate relationship. There were parts of her work that she loved. Working with the dresses, happy brides, deciding what to purchase for the shop, and other aspects of running her mother's business. On the other hand there was stress, keeping bills paid, bridezillas, and crazy wedding party members. She also had a nagging feeling there was something else out there she should be doing instead.

At least her mother had become more involved with the business, which was a blessing. It freed Madison up, but if Roman was in Chicago, she had a lot of time to herself. That never bothered her before as she worked on her designs, but the inspiration for designing had wilted. She needed to find a new passion to pursue.

Madison waved when she spotted Stephanie flipping the sign in the window to open. At least Stephanie knew what she wanted to be—a published writer. The art center already had some of her short stories and poems, but her goal was to eventually write full-time. When that day came, she'd miss her friend enormously.

"Hey, girl." Madison placed her coffee cup on the counter and wiggled out of her coat.

"Hi. How was your weekend?" Stephanie folded her arms across her chest. For some reason she'd never liked Roman and that was even before they knew he was the infamous mafia man they'd read about in the papers.

"Good. How about you?" Madison hung her coat in the closet, walked into her office, and flipped through the mail on her desk.

"Okay. I got some writing done." Her friend followed, stood on one foot, and twirled her finger around a long string of her blonde hair. It was a nervous habit she had and it almost always hinted there was something on her mind.

"And?" Madison raised her eyebrow but didn't look up.

"And what?" Stephanie placed her hands on her hips.

"Is there something wrong? I got a feeling that you want to ask me about something."

Her mouth opened but nothing came out. The door in the main room opened and an excited group of girls entered the store. "I'd better go." Stephanie excused herself and left to care for their customers.

With a shake of her head, Madison settled in

behind her desk. She really needed to talk to her friend and see what the problem was. In the back of her mind, there was also the nagging suspicion that it somehow involved Roman.

For the next half hour, Madison caught up on emails, voice mail, bills, and all the details for the upcoming fashion show. While she worked, a constant flow of customers came and went through the front entrance but Stephanie never asked for any help.

Tuning out the conversations in the other room, Madison kept her nose to the business at hand. She closed her eyes and yawned. When she opened her eyes, a tattooed finger tapped an envelope in front of her. The man placed his hand on the desk. Each digit was tattooed and tanned. Swallowing hard, her gaze slowly followed the length of his suit clad arm up to his cold, hard face.

It was him. Her breath caught and her pulse pounded in her ears. The beast who trashed her store.

"What do you want?" Her voice squeaked and she grabbed for her phone.

He was quicker and flung it across the room. It crashed against the wall and fell to the floor. The screen shattered.

"I'm here to help you." His statement and thick accent was confusing. Russian, possibly, but she couldn't tell. He put one finger to his lips. "*Shh.*" The guy straightened and then wandered around the room.

Madison sat up straight. "Who are you?"

"It's not important who I am. It is important who

157

I represent." All the oxygen seemed to flow from the room.

Her mind had to interpret what he meant moments after he said it. His words were hard to understand and truth be told, she feared for her life. How did he get past Stephanie? Panic set in. Where was Stephanie? Her gaze darted to the now closed door.

"Relax. The last time was a warning."

"Warning? Watch my back? I don't even know what that means."

"The warning wasn't for you. It was for him."

"Him who?" It was best to keep him talking while she figured out what to do. And where were the security people who watched the shop?

"Caponelli. You don't think he is really interested in you, some little girl from nowhere?"

Madison swallowed. Her heart broke in two. Was she just a pawn in some kind of mob war?

"He is trying to buy up the town and we want to beat him to it. That was a warning for him to back off."

"I don't understand." She swallowed.

"We want to develop this area. Romeo just wants to launder his illegal business through your legal ones."

Her head was spinning. She reached for some bottled water and took a drink.

"I am here to make you an offer from my boss." His pacing intimidated her as much as when he simply remained in one place. There seemed to be no one she could trust and something about him frightened her as much as Diego had.

"What kind of offer?" As soon as his back turned, she grabbed a letter opener from the desk and held it in her lap.

"My boss wishes to buy your property."

"He wants a bridal store?" That's the last thing she expected to hear.

"No, the property. He wants to tear it down and build bigger and better business." The word *wants* sounded like *vaunts*.

"I'm sorry, but I don't own the building. My mother does and I'm not sure when she will return." Not to mention the fact that she would never sell.

He stopped in front of her desk, picked up the envelope, and tossed it closer. "I know she is in town. The offer is in here." Mister Russian bully guy crossed his arms over his chest and laughed. "I suggest you take this one. The second offer will be less."

"What about the third one?" Her defiance and courage grew and she avoided looking at the letter as if it was an overdue bill.

"Those that don't take what's offered aren't around for a third one." He crossed the room and rested his hand on the doorknob. "I suggest you don't take too long. Have a good day, Miss Miller." *Good* came out as *goot*. The man waited for a response and she finally nodded. "I'll be in touch."

Chapter Eighteen

As soon as the door was closed, she rushed to lock it. Then Madison flew to the window. The goon walked down the sidewalk like he didn't have a care in the world. A black SUV waited. It was one very similar to the kind that Roman used but somehow different. She couldn't put her finger on what. A brief warning light flashed in her mind. Were they somehow connected?

Madison jumped when someone knocked on her door. "Yikes." She'd forgotten about Stephanie and rushed to open it.

"Are you okay?" They both spoke as the same time.

"Security just called," Stephanie added. "They'll be right here. Who was that guy?" Her words were flying out a hundred miles a minute. "I'm sorry. I must have been putting some dresses away in the fitting rooms. I never saw him come in, only leave. I was scared to death something had happened to you." She had a death grip on the iron and was on the cusp of freaking out.

"You were scared. I was terrified." The intimidation had radiated from him.

Stephanie narrowed her eyes. "So help me, if I see him again I will beat him to a pulp." The nasty scar on her face hadn't faded much.

"He never said who he worked for, just that he wanted to buy the building. He said the offer was in the envelope."

They both turned at the same time and regarded the letter like a viper.

"Is anyone still in the store?" Madison asked.

"No, they all left." Her voice shook.

In the next second, several of Roman's men swarmed the shop.

Madison whispered to Stephanie, "Don't say anything about the letter."

It sat untouched on the desk while the guys took down their story of what happened and promised to watch from a car out front in case he came back. There was also a big guy in a suit camped out in the front room. Having him there was a comfort but she wasn't sure how they would explain his presence to their customers.

Stephanie never questioned her request to remain quiet. Wiping her sweaty palms on her sweater, Madison stepped up to the desk and ripped the letter open. It was indeed an offer to buy the building. A reasonable offer, but there was no way her mother would sell the building. There was also a deadline to let them know.

"Who's it from?" Stephanie's exotic perfume tickled her nose as she looked over her shoulder.

Madison flipped the letter over and checked both

sides of the envelope. Nothing.

"It doesn't say. It just says they'll be in touch." Goosebumps raced up her arm.

They both jerked as the phone in the other room rang.

"I'll get it," Stephanie said.

Madison hugged herself as she contemplated her next move. She would, of course, have to notify her mother, wherever she may be at the moment. At least Connie was in town somewhere.

"What?" Stephanie's exclamation rang loud, and Madison wandered out from the office.

She held the phone in one hand and her finger wrapped around her hair with the other.

"Okay, let me know what happens." Stephanie hung up the phone and collapsed in a nearby chair.

"What is it?" The day was going downhill fast.

"That was Andrea over at the arts center." Andrea had been the shy, quiet bride that Madison helped get away from her abusive fiancée. It had taken a while to get her out and about, and working at the center had done wonders for her. Unfortunately, she still had a long way to go before she would ever trust men again.

"Is something wrong?" The poor girl had been through so much.

"Apparently that jerk just made a visit there too."

"He didn't hurt Andrea, did he?" She pressed her shaky hand to her chest.

"No, fortunately there were other people there at the time. He just gave her the letter and left." Exhaling, Madison collapsed in a chair and the phone rang again. She locked eyes with Stephanie as she answered it and there was no need to hear what was said on the other end to know it was no good. After the conversation ended, Stephanie sat quietly.

"Who was that?" Madison leaned forward and rested her elbows on her knees.

"The couple that owns the Chinese restaurant. Big, scary guy was there too."

The phone rang a few more times with the same story.

A chill eased its way up her arm. Roman promised to never do anything to change her town, but questions niggled at her mixed with fear. All these businesses were ones they'd visited in the last few weeks. They were also places Roman mentioned should be developed.

"You know I don't want to say this, but do you think Caponelli has a hand in this?" Her friend even had a hard time saying his name. "I mean, how did this guy get in here with the security system?"

"Stephanie, you've had a problem with Roman since we met. Is there something you aren't telling me?"

"No. I know his kind and you don't need someone like that in your life." She looked her straight in the eye. "Look at what's happening already. Directly or indirectly, he has caused this."

"What should I do? I can't believe he would have any connection to this." It didn't make sense. Was he behind this somehow but making it look like it was someone else? Bullying her and others she cared about into selling their businesses would only put a wedge in their relationship, not make it stronger. Had she been a pawn all along?

"I don't know what to tell you, but we've got to do something and fast before whoever it is buys the whole damn town."

"Madison?" Roman's voiced roared from the other room before he rushed into her office. "Thank God." He crushed her to his chest in a big hug. "Are you all right? I heard what happened and broke every speed limit to get here."

"Yes, I'm fine. Shaken up a bit."

"Tony." Roman let her go and went to drill the man left behind in the main room. For a tough guy working security, even he appeared rattled at Roman's attention. "What the hell happened? You guys are supposed to be watching day and night."

Tony tugged at his collar. "We were. It wasn't until we noticed no traffic or movement after a few minutes that we realized the surveillance had been stalled. These guys are good. They must have hacked into the system and froze the camera shots right before the guy entered."

"Son of a bitch. I want this guy's head on a platter."

"Yes, boss. We already have the IT guy checking the whole system out."

"Keep working on it and let me know as soon as they have something."

"You got it." Tony dialed up his phone to check on any progress as Roman ushered her back into the office.

Arlo walked in the front door and followed them as well. "I know you have probably answered all the guys questions a hundred times already, but is there anything at all that you remember about this guy?"

"What I mentioned before. His height, the tattoos, the accent." She exhaled and wandered to the window. "Wait a minute." She paused and her mind worked, searching for the missing piece.

"What is it?" Roman was at her side.

"I saw his vehicle."

"You didn't happen to get a license plate number, did you?"

"No, but I did notice something odd."

"What?"

Everyone in the room was staring at her, holding their breath. "It's probably nothing, but he was in one of those big black SUVs. You know, the kind you drive...only different."

"Different how?"

"I think it was a Ford." Roman used Cadillacs. "And there was something else. Dark hub caps...black."

"Black?"

"Yes, I'm sure of it. I knew there was something odd, but couldn't put a figure on it until now."

"Arlo?" Roman addressed his enforcer.

"Already on it." His man was out the door in a flash. The guy was itching to hurt someone and it was only a matter of time before he did.

"I'm so sorry you had to go through this again. We will find this guy, I promise." He held her tight. The moment he stepped into the shop, she knew he wasn't responsible. Roman may be a big tough guy, but she'd seen genuine relief when his eyes met hers. "If anyone dares to ever lay hands on you again, I *swear* I will kill them with mine." Venom sounded in his voice as he held up his large, tanned hands.

"It's okay. I know they'll find him." Madison laid her head on his neck as he held her close. His fingers stroked her hair.

She had her moments of doubt, but every time he was close those uncertainties slipped away. In her heart, she knew he would hunt down anyone who harmed her and that he *would* kill them. In her heart, she knew she loved him no matter what he did.

Chapter Nineteen

Roman

Rinaldi and his father would have to wait. He'd called both yesterday and cancelled his trip to Chicago to keep an eye on Madison. He also had to make tracks to Milwaukee again. Arlo was in the driver's seat and they were in the center car of a convoy of three. In all the chaos, he'd forgotten to give her the ring.

The shipment of cars was in, as well as the merchandise contained in them. The buyers were there as well. Then it was off to meet the Fenetti family. Oscar had insisted again that it was the Rinaldis who were making waves but they thought they could handle it. If they needed help, they would let them know. Roman didn't bring it up in his phone call to Bruno, but if the stories were true, he would make his suspicions known.

"After we stop at the car dealership in Milwaukee and check on the cars, we have a meeting with the Fenettis." If things were missed, shit got messy. Diego's death was on the tip of it. This should have ended as soon as the fucker's skull had hit the ground. No one but Madison, his father, and the men who were there knew he'd killed the asshole. Word on the street was that the Rinaldi family suspected they had something to do with his 'disappearance' but he had a hard time believing they were involved with the warehouse fire and other small time shit.

Diego was a menace. The Rinaldis were probably ecstatic that the douchebag was gone, but it would show weakness if they didn't claim restitution of some kind for the death of one of their members, even if the guy was a psychopath. Until they came out and made their demands known, Roman was laying low.

In the back of his mind, he knew that was part of the reason his father was pushing the marriage to Layla, but there was only one woman he would take as his wife. He picked up his phone and placed a call.

"Val, how's it going?"

"Good, the place looks amazing."

He snorted. "I could give a rat's ass about decorations. I want to know if you've found anything out."

His sister's loud exhale echoed in the phone. "Give me a second to get to the office." He waited as she hurried to the room for more privacy. "I checked all land and business purchases in the past few months and only one stands out as odd. It's a corporation called Coalition Inc. They purchased a property along the lake, but no one has moved into it. They ordered a $350,000 wood hull boat from Sunseeker Boatworks. Tomorrow, I'm going to stop in and see if I can get the name of who signed for it."

"Call me as soon as you have that name."

"Do you want to talk to Madison now?"

"You bet your ass I do," he said.

"Hold on."

He could hear her leave the room and call to his woman. "Here she is."

"Hey, beautiful." He wished he could see her face.

"Hello." Madison's cheerful voice warmed his heart.

"I'm headed to town for some meetings."

"Well, be careful."

"I always am, sweetheart. Anything you need me to bring you back?"

"There is something I could use."

"Name it." He'd do anything for her.

"The Mr. Mouse Cheese Factory still isn't cleared for that salmonella outbreak. I need lots of cheese trays and a model."

He chuckled. "That's two things."

"Are you up for the challenge?"

"Done. I know a guy."

Madison

Madison floated on air. The whole day was perfect. Never had a bridal event gone off as well as this one. Usually by now, she'd have pulled out several pieces of hair and gnawed off at least three fingernails.

This was the first time she'd been able to watch the show. Valentina had been a great help. She arranged for some of the female staff at Firenza to help with dressing the models and there wasn't much else for her to do. Even Roman had held up his end of the bargain. He hired the Gessners, an old family friend and cheese maker, to do the hors d'oeuvres. Their daughter was her newest model.

Madison rested against the back wall and watched the show. Stephanie stood to the right of the temporary stage and read the gown descriptions for the models' dresses. Kai, the girl Roman found, was up now. Her face beamed as she walked to the end of the runway and did a perfect turn. The beads and sequins of her gown sparkled in the lights. Madison had met her parents before the show as they set out their cheese selections along the buffet. Her taste buds still sang with all the different kinds she'd tested. Each one was more appetizing than the last.

If the buzz around the buffet table was any indication, Firenza would be a popular, if not, the number one place on many bridal reception lists. It wasn't just the brides who were excited. Several of the photographers who had booths there today were asking about having photo shoots on the site. A local florist also wanted in on the act and was already courting Valentina about providing fresh flowers and landscaping for Firenza from one of their partners.

Despite the last minute changes, things couldn't be better. Madison leaned against the back wall and studied the faces of the crowd. Mothers and daughters, grandmothers and granddaughters, nieces and aunts—everyone seemed to be enjoying the event. Business would be booming this week with brides-to-be walking in with their favorite dresses circled in the program.

A melancholy shadow hovered like a cloud on her perfect day. Tomorrow she'd be traveling to Chicago to meet Roman's parents. Why now and why so soon in their relationship? Roman said he knew what he wanted and what he wanted was her. If only she could be so sure.

Chicago had her stomach in knots. Being in a big city would be claustrophobic and anxiety set in. Heck, going to Chicago to order dresses at the fall and spring buyers' shows left her counting the minutes until she could go home.

At only thirty years old, she was in a rut. Madison was young enough to still be restless and eager for adventure, yet old enough to already have too many responsibilities to do anything about it. Every time Roman was with her, the doubts disappeared. When they were together, anything seemed possible.

Madison studied the crowd. It wasn't the potential customers she was searching for. Her eyes were magnets for him. He wasn't hard to find. Even if he wasn't in a room of mostly women, his tall frame would be easy to spot anywhere. Roman was deep in conversation with his right hand man, Arlo. She couldn't help but let her thoughts stray to mafia type business. She exhaled deeply. The man was involved in organized crime.

Like a fire on a dark night, she couldn't tear her gaze away. Where Roman was concerned there was no one else, no one more intriguing, and no one she'd rather be with. She had always been the good girl, the sweet girl. The one who never got into trouble. But where did that get her? Roman was now deep in conversation across the room with Mr. Gessner and he laughed at something he said. His body language was relaxed and to anyone who didn't know who he was, the man would appear to be any normal guy from the community.

Roman may appear calm and collected, but it was a pretty good bet he had a least one gun under that fancy suit of his. The cheesemaker standing next to him probably shopped at the local department store. Roman's navy suit had been custom made in Chicago and probably cost more than what she made in a month. The burgundy shirt he wore highlighted his dark complexion. He was sporting a day's worth of stubble, making her want to purr like a cat.

The crowd's applause covered her groan—or was it a moan?—as she remembered their erotic night. As if on cue, Roman turned her way. His eyes lingered on hers for a moment before he made a sweeping glance from her head to her toes. Even from a distance, heat followed the movement of his eyes, warming her from the inside out. Returning his attention to the man in front of him, Roman shook his hand in a very businesslike manner and headed her way. She used the program to cool her heated face.

"Congratulations." His bright smile never failed

to leave her short of breath. "I'd say this was a huge success."

Before she could get a word out, Madison was bombarded with questions from brides and Stephanie grasped her arm. All she could do was nod before being whisked away and surrounded by prospective customers and clients. The wives-to-be were the easiest. She handed out cards and invited them to stop in and try on their favorite picks from the fashion show. Several other venders from the show said they would stop in the following week with business cards and displays. The Gessners talked about giving discounts on cheese and meat trays for those who purchased dresses from Madison.

As things finally started to wind down, she was able to process everything that had happened. All in all, it was her best event ever. Would things have been as successful if they'd stayed at the same place? Probably not. Firenza brought new excitement and new clients to the show.

It seemed like forever before the entire crowd was gone. The dresses then needed to be bagged up, packed into a van, and returned to the store. Out of nowhere, a group of young men were there to carry everything to the vehicle. That never happened at the other venue. She'd been furious at Roman for the stunt he pulled, but it had definitely been to her benefit in the long run.

"Is there anything else you need help with?"

"*Augh*." The stack of business cards in her hand went flying, breaking her deep thought while her hands flew to her chest. "You scared me half to death! What are you, part ninja?"

"Sorry." He bent to gather the cards. "Like I was saying before you were pulled away, congratulations on the event. I can't say that I've ever been to something like this before, but it was very well organized and it looks like all involved will be getting an enormous amount of business out of it." Roman still held all the cards, in more ways than one. "Valentina has already booked several wedding receptions."

"Yes, we were lucky to get this many people here after having to change locations at the last minute."

"It's a small town. Word gets out."

"Word would have gotten out much better if we hadn't had to change locations." She jabbed him in the ribs. He was not going to get off easy for being deceptive. If they were going to be in a relationship, everything would have to be out in the open. The good and the bad.

"Then I guess we should have announced that it will be held here each year from now on."

Her fists settled to her waist even though she melted at the sight of him. Of course it would be great to have it here every year, but that was for her to decide.

"You may be able to push everyone else around, Mr. Caponelli, but you won't push me." She poked him playfully in the chest.

"Have I told you how beautiful you are when you have fire in your eyes?"

Madison snatched the cards from his hand. Just the brief contact with his warm skin caused her cheeks to flush. It was getting harder and harder to say no to him about anything when all she wanted was to say yes.

Even words escaped her when he was around. Her normal assertive self became mush.

Roman raised an eyebrow, waiting for her response.

"Be careful you don't get too close to the fire, you might get burned." She tilted her head, raised her shoulder, and narrowed her eyes.

His robust laugh both thrilled and irked at the same time. "I will gladly risk that." His gaze scanned her from head to toe.

Madison folded her arms across her chest and tapped the sole of her shoe on the tile floor. She was backed into a corner where he was concerned. His nearness had her yearn for more, yet his chosen profession had her wanting to flee to a witness protection program. They had a lot to work through, but it seemed not to matter as much anymore.

Her back was against the hard wood of the hallway entrance where she had been gathering the brochures and literature left from the show. His expensive cologne intoxicated her senses with outdoorsy smells of cedar and balsam as he rested his palm on the paneling near her head. Madison exhaled and his dark eyes lowered to her breasts before returning to her gaze.

"So what time should I pick you up?"

She frowned. "Pick me up for what?"

He placed his other hand over his heart. "Have you forgotten so soon?"

What is he talking about?

"Our date." Roman had promised to take her out to dinner after the show.

She hadn't forgotten but being in his presence tended to cause her to lose all train of thought.

"I'm kind of tired." She tried to brush him off. "I'm too exhausted to even cook."

"I'll cook." Roman took his palms off the wall and shoved both hands in his pockets. He looked both pleased and excited, like a little boy eager to show off his skills.

"I know you can cook spaghetti but what else can you cook? Somehow I can't picture mob boss Romeo Caponelli in an apron." Madison rested her spine along the wall and set her fists on her hips. This she had to see.

"I'm an underboss," he corrected. "And I'm Italian so of course I can cook. We love to eat." His smile was contagious. "Haven't you ever noticed that when a mob boss gets killed he's in or around a restaurant?"

He was joking but the image of Roman lying on some cold sidewalk surrounded in blood chilled her to the bone. Her fingers automatically covered her mouth.

"I'm sorry." He took her hand in his. "A poor joke. I didn't mean to upset you, but I hope that by your response it would bother you if something were to happen to me."

"Of course it would. I don't want anything bad to happen to anyone. That's one of the reasons I didn't want to get involved with you."

"Nothing's going to happen to me," he declared.

"You can't guarantee that," she countered and

stared at the ground.

"No one can guarantee that." He lifted her chin with his finger. "I don't mean to bring up sad memories, but didn't your father pass away before you were born? People die in car accidents, get cancer, and fall in the bathtub." Images of their scuffle in her bathroom came to mind. "But that doesn't mean we shouldn't love them."

He was right but she still had her reservations about dating a mob boss—make that underboss. Heck, she didn't even know what the difference was, but it was true. *We don't know how many days we have on earth.* Just the heat from his finger was warming her from the inside out. Taking a deep breath, she pushed away from the wall and smiled.

"You win, Mr. Underboss. I'll have dinner with you tonight." Madison strutted down the hallway before turning. "We'll see how good a cook you are." She may be tired, but the man had a way of getting under her skin and making her feel alive.

"Great. And by the way, since the show is over with, I want to take you to meet my parents tomorrow," Roman added before heading off in the other direction.

His parents? A lump lodged in her throat.

Chapter Twenty

Madison snuggled into the warm seats and closer to the handsome man next to her in the backseat of the SUV. They may be traveling south, but the closer she got to Chicago, the colder she felt. They'd shared a nice dinner at his home the night before and she'd spent the night again. The guy was an addiction. Never in her life had she met some man's parents before. The thought that he was the son of a powerful mob boss made the stress even greater.

What if they didn't like her? Would she be sporting cement stilettoes and tossed into Lake Michigan?

"What's wrong?" Roman woke her from her day dreaming.

"Just a little nervous I guess." It was the truth, but it was more than a little.

"Don't worry. I love you, Valentina loves you, and everyone at dinner will love you." He kissed her hard. The passion took the edge off her fright and replaced it with desire. The guy could throw her off balance with a glance.

"Wait a second." She sat up straighter and played with the belt of her coat. "Did you just say you loved me?"

"Of course I did." He hit the button to close off their section of the vehicle from Arlo and the driver in the front seat. "From the moment I saw you at the Snowflake Ball, I fell for you. The way you moved across the dance floor. The way your hair came loose when you spun around. I was transfixed, under your spell. I've had many women, Madison, but you're the only one I've ever loved. When you were kidnapped, I couldn't breathe until I knew you were safe." He reached in his pocket and pulled out a box.

Her heart beat so loud, it would surely jump from her chest.

"It's not an engagement ring. I know it's too soon for that, but I know what I want and what I want is you." He opened the box and took out a vintage style sapphire ring. "It's a promise ring." He picked up her left hand and slipped it on her shaking finger. "I promise to be true to you. Honor you and always protect you."

"I don't know what to say." Her voice came out as a whisper. It was hard to catch her breath. Was this really happening?

"You don't have to say anything. Just wearing it tells me everything I need to know." He kissed her hand and held it in his lap.

"It's beautiful." The ring was perfect and something that she would have picked out for herself. He definitely knew her style already. "I love it." She kissed his cheek.

The vehicle stopped and her breathing accelerated. They were here.

***

The Caponelli home was even bigger than Roman's Genoa one. She'd get lost for sure if she was left to wander on her own.

Despite her worries, his family was very welcoming. It seemed like there was a black cloud hanging over the otherwise great day. Valentina was bubbly and kept the conversation flowing. His mother, Celine, was very gracious and asked a lot of questions about Genoa and her bridal store. Madison filled with pride at the interest she showed.

Roman's father, on the other hand, scared the crap out of her. The man didn't say much during the meal at all and whenever he glanced her way, there was a look of disapproval.

"Thank you for this wonderful meal. It was fabulous." Madison dabbed her mouth with a silk napkin, careful to not leave any lipstick on the luxurious cloth.

"Well, I hope you saved room for Cherries Jubilee. It's our cook's specialty."

"We have to go back to Genoa tonight, but we have time for that." Roman smiled.

"It sounds heavenly." Even though she was stuffed, there was no way she'd pass up that dish.

"Let's have dessert and coffee in the family room." His mother stood up and everyone followed.

"We will join you shortly," his father stated. "I

need to speak with Roman in my office." It was the first time he'd talked and the sense of doom grew darker.

"I will be with you soon." Roman kissed her cheek and the two men left the room.

"Come with me." Valentina grabbed her arm and they trailed after the others. "Is everything okay?"

"Yes, just a little nervous."

"Nothing to be nervous about," Valentina assured her.

She was ushered into the family room and soon enchanted with family photos. The ones of Roman as a child made her beam. It was easy to picture him as a little boy sneaking cookies from the kitchen and getting away with mischief with a simple smile and a wink.

"Valentina?" she whispered. "Where is the bathroom?"

"Oh, just take a right, then a left, and it's the second door."

"Thanks. I'll be right back."

There were more family photos in the long hallway, including a huge painting of an elderly couple. His grandparents, perhaps? Madison strolled down the hall and before long was lost. All the doors looked the same. What was it again? Right, left…left, right?

Up ahead, she heard voices. One she recognized as Roman's and the other was that of his father. Thankfully, they would get her to the restroom and back for dessert.

As she neared, the voices escalated and her steps slowed. They were obviously not in agreement about something.

"I don't care what you think," Roman stated. "I will not marry someone I don't love."

Were they talking about her? Madison held her breath.

"You don't have a choice," his father countered. "I made an agreement with Rinaldi and you must abide by it or else."

"You made the pact, I didn't."

"And you must follow it." Madison jumped as she heard what sounded like a fist hit a desk. "It is a good match. A Caponelli must marry a Rinaldi or there will be war and you will be the cause of it."

Roman cursed and could be heard pacing the room. "I won't do it. I'm in love with Madison."

"And she seems like a wonderful girl. Keep her as your mistress, I don't care, but if you don't follow through and marry Rinaldi blood, you will no longer be my son."

"Do you know what you are asking me?"

"I do and I expect you to follow my orders." Even from the hallway, she could tell he meant business.

"And if I don't?"

"Don't make me do that." His father's voice cracked. "You know what happens. What has to happen to those who go against me."

"I'd rather die than have to marry someone else." Roman's voice was getting closer to the door and she sank back in the shadows.

"If you don't marry her, you will."

Madison saw stars. Did she hear right? Roman was being forced to marry some girl from another mafia family or there would be some kind of sick war, and if he didn't do as he was told, they would kill him. Was this the dark ages?

He would refuse to do it. She knew he would and because of her, he would die. As much as she loved him, she couldn't let that happened. The ring on her finger felt like lead and tears threatened to fall.

"Madison? Were you looking for me?" Roman had stepped out into the hallway after slamming the door behind him.

"Ah, no. I was looking for the bathroom." She turned her head back in the direction she came. "I'm afraid I got lost."

"Don't worry. It's two doors down." He hugged her tight. "I want to go home now. I'll have the cook dish our desserts up to go and say our farewells."

"All right. I'll be right there," she mumbled.

It felt rude to leave in a hurry, but she no longer felt welcome. She wandered into the restroom and shut the door. Her heart was breaking off piece by piece, like a flower losing its petals.

There was no choice. She had to break it off and save his life.

The whole way home was a blur. Roman's father's voice kept replaying in her mind.

"Are you sure everything's all right?" Roman asked for the third time.

"Yes." It was dark, but she stared out the window the whole time.

"You don't seem fine. You've barely said a word since we left."

"I'm just tired." The car turned toward Roman's

home and she panicked. "Arlo, please take me to my home."

"What?" Roman turned her way.

"I want to go home."

"Whatever you need, we have at the house."

"I want to go home. Now."

"All right." He finally caved in. "Arlo, take us to Madison's. We can spend the night there."

She gritted her teeth. He wasn't going to make this easy. In just minutes, they were parked out front of her door.

Arlo opened her car door and she was out in a flash. Roman quickly followed and grabbed her arm. "What the hell is going on?"

"I can't do this."

"Do what?" he demanded.

"I can't be with you. I don't belong in your world." She pulled the ring from her finger and held it out. When he refused to take it, she dropped it in his coat pocket.

"I don't understand."

"I'm sorry, but this has to end before someone gets hurt." Madison stepped around him and continued to her doorstep.

"What do you mean? Everything's been going great."

"It's not great anymore. I'm sorry, but I don't want to see you anymore." She struggled to get the key in the lock. "Please don't contact me again."

"What the hell?" Shock was written all over his face and it hurt her more. She didn't want to break it off, but if it kept him alive it would be worth it. A pit formed in her stomach. The realization that she loved him made it even worse.

"The show's over. I don't need you anymore." The look on his face turned from shock to hurt to anger.

"I don't know what kind of game you are playing, but I know you don't mean that."

"I do." It was a lie and her eyes brimmed with tears. She'd never been a good liar. It was a relief to finally be in her home.

"We need to talk." He followed her in.

"No, we don't. Thanks for everything, but whatever you thought we had is over. Please leave." The brave face she'd put on was going to crumble any minute if he didn't leave soon. It took all she had not to rush into his arms and apologize. She wanted to admit she was only doing it to keep him from being killed, but that would never do.

What kind of evil father would have his son murdered for not marrying the one he wanted him to? The kind of family she didn't need to be involved with anyway. It might take forever or it might never happen again, but she had to put Roman's life first. If she never got married or fell in love again, so be it.

Roman's jaw muscles flexed and he glared at her. "You obviously aren't going to tell me what has changed. I'm leaving, but this isn't over. Not by a long shot." He marched to the door, threw it open, and slammed it shut.

Madison hurried to lock it behind him. Not only to keep him out but to keep her from rushing after him.

Chapter Twenty One

Roman

The next few days were miserable. Roman had hit the gym and pounded the punching bag often. He now sat in his office tapping a pencil on the desk. What the hell had happened? Tossing the pencil across the room, he ran his fingers through his hair while trying to figure out what went wrong. So far, Madison had refused to return his calls and he was certainly not going to go over there and beg.

His cell phone buzzed.

"Hello."

"Romeo, I've got something for you." It was Valentina.

"What?"

"The guy you're looking for."

"Oh, yeah. I forgot."

"Geez, Roman, what's wrong with you? I thought you'd be excited."

"I am. I've just got a lot on my mind." He slid in his chair.

"Have you heard from Madison?"

"No."

There was a pause on the line. "Do you want me to talk to her? Girl to girl and see what's going on."

"No. I want you to tell me what you found so I can go break some bones." It was just want he needed.

"Okay, okay. I'm sending you a message right now with what I've found, both at the boat builder's and the real estate office. I made copies of everything." He checked his email while they talked. It was a name he recognized. It did and it didn't make sense, but the man would confess his reasons before Roman was done with him and he would relish dealing out his punishment. Finally, the solution to who was responsible for the problems in town and a chance to work off the tension from being apart from the love of his life.

"Got it. Thanks, Val. I owe you."

"Save it. Just get the bastard and then get your woman back. I don't care what Father says, you can't marry someone just for the sake of the family."

Roman ran copies off on the printer. "I got to go." He hung up and grabbed his coat. There was a lot to do.

"Arlo," Roman yelled and headed for the kitchen.

"Yeah, boss." Arlo ran into him in the hallway. "I was just coming to get you."

"Call Dom and get the men together. We have a lot to do." Roman kept moving as he barked out orders.

187

"Ah, boss, there's something—"

"I don't want to hear about it. I want to take care of this. Now."

"But, boss, there's someone here to see you." They rounded the corner and a young woman stood in the entryway. "Miss Layla Rinaldi is here to speak to you." Arlo pointed to the obvious.

What is she doing here? Her stunning resemblance to Madison irked him even more. He couldn't think of marrying someone that appeared so much like the one he loved. It would be a stab to the heart with a dull blade every time he looked at her.

"Mr. Caponelli." She stepped forward and held out her hand. "We need to talk."

"Of course." Roman directed his attention to Arlo. "Do as I say and I will be with you shortly. Right this way, Miss Rinaldi."

Layla fidgeted as she sat in a chair opposite Roman on the other side of his desk. She wrung her hands before she spoke.

"I can't do this."

"Can't do what?" Roman scowled at the woman in front of him. It was misplaced, but he felt it all the same. She wasn't the problem. They were both in a situation that they didn't want to be in.

"You know very well what I mean. This fake marriage to join our families."

Roman took a deep breath and rested his elbows on the desk.

"I'm not a piece of property to be traded. You can't be serious about following through with this farce," she continued.

188

"It means death if I don't marry you."

Layla's mouth dropped open.

"You can't tell me you don't know that," he said. "Are you asking me to back out so that you can get off free? Neither of us has the easy answer."

"I lied to my father to come here."

Roman echoed her frustration.

A long silence stretched before Layla continued. "I'm sorry he's doing this."

"It's not your fault." He waved her apology away.

"I should go." She stood up. Her face was a mask of despair as she spun to leave. "I told him I'd be shopping in town. I'd better go do that. He probably has people watching me."

Roman's anger melted at her frustration and he stood too.

"Layla, wait."

She stopped and turned to look directly at Roman. They were both victims here and she didn't deserve his anger.

"I know this is not what we both want. Hopefully, we can make the best of it. Whatever that may be." Even he wasn't convinced of that, but she didn't need to know that. The situation weighed heavy on her too.

Layla nodded and a few strands of hair covered her face. He should have been more understanding, but he wasn't. She shouldn't be here and there was too much to do.

Roman showed Layla out and she seemed a little more relaxed. It was as if they had both become resigned to the fact that this was happening. As soon as she left, Roman headed straight to the bar in the living room. A drink would clear his mind, maybe two. Neither one of them wanted to be shackled to another in a phony marriage. There was no disagreement on that.

***

Roman's phone buzzed as he rode in the car with Arlo and two of his other men. It was Dominic.

"He's not here," Dom said. "The hotel clerk said he'd just checked out."

"Dammit. Keep asking around. See if anyone knows where he might have gone."

Dom disconnected the call. There was no need to answer. The man was a blood hound. He wouldn't stop until he found his target, the man with the tattooed fingers who had threatened Madison.

Arlo had also been on his phone at the same time. "Roman, there's been an explosion."

"Where?"

"A car bomb across from Bells and Bows."

A pit formed in his gut. "Was anyone hurts?"

"Doesn't appear so, but the car belonged to one of the other business owners that was threatened the same day as Madison by this guy." Arlo held up the photo that Valentina had sent over with the guy's stats. No wonder the man had left town and Dom couldn't find him.

"I want this guy dead." Roman hit his fist against the door. "Drive over there. I want to make sure Madison's okay."

The car made a U-turn and headed for Madison's

shop. If anyone touched her, he would skin them alive.

A crowd had gathered out front and the police were now on the scene. He rolled his eyes when he saw Officer Donovan motioning people back. They drove past the chaos and parked a block away. Cautiously, they approached the burning car. He searched the crowd hoping to spot the guy who did it. So often the person responsible stayed behind to watch the aftermath of their crime, but he was nowhere to be found.

"Damn," he said. Dominic needed to find the muscle man before he hurt someone.

Exhaling, he turned his attention to Bells and Bows and his eyes met Madison's. The woman drove him crazy. How dare she turn him down after he gave her his ring and his undying love? He didn't believe for a minute that she'd used him. There was something else going on and when he was done with his enemy, they would talk. Roman never took no for an answer.

"Roman," a woman yelled, and ran into his arms. It was Layla.

"It was awful," she said. "I just walked by and it blew up." She was shaking like a leaf.

"Are you all right?" He disengaged himself from her hold. No blood or burns could be seen.

She stepped back and glanced down at her clothes. "Yes, but I could feel the heat. It was that close."

"Arlo." He turned to his bodyguard. "Take care of Layla."

"Of course." He ushered her to their car.

When Roman glanced back at the bridal shop, Madison was gone. He swore and then grimaced as he spied Donovan walking his way.

"Mr. Caponelli, I'd like you to come down to the station with me."

"What for?"

Another officer now stood by his side.

"I'd like to ask you a few questions."

As if the day couldn't get any worse.

"Anything you say." Roman sighed and followed Ryan to his car. He sent a text to the men and that this late in the day, things were going to have to wait.

Thankfully, Madison was nowhere in sight. All he needed was for her to see him get into the back seat of a police car. Son of a bitch, could something go right today?

***

Madison

As hard as she tried, Madison couldn't get rid of the image of the woman in Roman's arms. It sure didn't take him long to find someone else. And the fact that the woman's appearance was so close to hers didn't help. Wow, how easily she could be replaced.

"Steph, I'm going home." Madison's stomach jolted, wanting to expel anything in it.

"What? Are you okay?"

"Yes, why?"

"You never leave early." Her eyes were wide.

"Well, my mother is back in town. I'll have her come over."

"It's not that. I'm just worried about you." Her friend dropped what she was doing and walked to her side. "I may not like Roman, but I know you do. It's hurts to see you so upset."

"It wasn't meant to be. I wanted a family man, not a man in a mafia family."

"We don't choose the ones we fall in love with."

"Since when are you on Roman's side? I thought you hated him."

Her friend shrugged. "I don't hate him. I was just concerned, and now you can see why. He's a complicated man and this is a complicated situation."

"I guess so. Everything's a mess right now, and what about the explosion outside? I'm worried about leaving you alone."

"Arlo phoned and said they'll have security stationed outside the rest of the day. No one will get in here that we don't want to get in."

Yes, this was complicated. She'd told Roman off and yet he was still paying for staff to keep an eye on their place. A headache threatened. "I need to go home. I'm not feeling too well."

Stephanie hugged her. "Don't worry, everything will work out. I know it."

Madison wiped away the tears before they could fall. "I know." She avoided looking Steph in the eye as she turned to gather her purse and keys. "I'm going home. See you tomorrow."

"Try to relax. See you."

As Madison left, some new customers came in.

Guilt was already filtering in for abandoning her job.

She'd barely stepped into her house when the doorbell rang. Madison peeked through the window. It was her mother.

"Hi, Mom."

Connie entered and threw her purse on the nearby couch. "Stephanie called."

"Really? What for?"

"To tell me that you left the store early." The expression on her face was one of concern.

"So, I left. What's wrong with that?"

"It's not like you."

"How would you know?" she snapped, and her mother frowned. "I'm sorry. I didn't mean that."

"Yes, you did, and I agree. I've not been here when you needed me most and that is going to change." Connie wandered over to the couch and took a seat. "Sit down, Maddy. I want to know what's wrong and what I can do to help."

Madison laughed. "There's nothing you or anyone can do to help."

"There's always something that can be done. Steph said Roman gave you a ring but you gave it back. I thought you liked the man."

"I do, but he's committed to marrying someone else." Her lower lip trembled.

"What?" Her mother jumped to her feet.

"Yeah, it's some mafia thing that his father set up. He's supposed to marry the daughter of some Rinaldi guy to make up for some injustice that was done to the family or something like that." Madison blew her nose on a tissue.

194

"What did you say?" Her mother gripped Madison's arms like her life depended on it.

"That he's supposed to marry some other girl or they'll kill him. That's why I broke it off. If he doesn't marry the daughter of Bruno Rinaldi, he'll be killed because he went against the family. It's barbaric." She waved her hand in the air.

Her mother's face went white.

"I know, I never should have gotten involved with him, but I couldn't help it. I love him." She sobbed and collapsed on the couch. Her mother's arms were now cradled around her and they rocked back and forth together.

Connie sighed loudly and pulled her daughter away so she could look her in the face.

"Listen to me and listen good. We don't always fall for the ones we should, but no one, and I repeat, *no one* is going to tell my daughter who she can or can't marry."

"No one told me I couldn't marry him, but when I overheard that he would be murdered if we did get married, I just couldn't do it. " Her sobs continued. "I know we haven't known each other long, but I know in my heart we were meant to be together."

"And together you two shall be." Connie stood up and grabbed her purse.

"What are you talking about? It's a done deal." Madison cried.

"A long time ago, I fell for your father. A guy I shouldn't have fallen for, but I loved him with all my heart. I let someone convince me that he wasn't the one. I am not going to let that happen to you." Connie marched to the door.

"Where are you going?"

"To set things right." And with a slam of the door, her mother was gone.

Madison shook her head, completely heartbroken. She dragged herself off the couch and into the bathroom. A hot bath and a glass of wine was all she could muster.

Chapter Twenty-Two

Roman

"What a fucking mess," Roman mumbled as he punched the bag again, hard.

He'd been tied up for hours at the police station answering stupid questions about where he had been when the car had blown up. Since they didn't have any leads, they were targeting him, looking at the wrong man. Unfortunately, Roman couldn't tell them the real guy behind it all because when that bastard went missing, they could tie it back to him. Nothing would stop him from bringing this fucker down. No one messed with his town and his woman. *No one!*

He hugged the bag to his chest. In a short time, the small town had grown on him. He wanted to keep it the way it was as much as Madison did. If that meant he had to kill anyone who wanted to destroy it, he would. The thug was trying to buy up all the businesses by threatening people and then he would turn around and sell them to the highest bidders. It was also in his plan to open a strip joint and other cover businesses to move drugs in and out. It would flip the town and run the good people out. This asshole had to go, and tonight, he would.

Arlo strolled into the gym.

"Everything is set for tonight and Dom's already got everything in place."

Roman gave the bag one more revenge-filled hit.

"I'm going to shower and then we'll go."

Leaving his fitness room, Roman grabbed his cell phone. He knew that Madison was at home. The guy assigned to watch her said she'd left the shop early, gone home, and hadn't left. The only activity had been her mother visiting briefly and hurrying away with tires burning rubber. It wouldn't surprise Roman if they were arguing.

His finger hovered over the call button. He was good at what he did, but there was always a chance he wouldn't come back alive, and he needed to hear her again.

The call connected.

"Hello." Just the sound of her voice caused his pulse to race.

"Madison."

"Yes." Her reply came out like a cry filled squeak.

"I wanted…" This was harder than all the bad shit he'd ever done in his whole life. To hear her voice did something to his insides. It made an ugly monster with a sympathetic heart well up from his stomach and claw at his throat.

"Wanted what?"

"To make sure you were okay." There was so much to say and he struggled to find any words.

"I'm okay."

A sob echoed on the line and the *monster* winced.

"I'm glad you are all right."

Again there was silence.

"I have to go." He choked as he remembered the words she spoke to him when she broke things off. "I love you, Madison."

"Roman, I…" She sniffled and it was agony to his ears.

"You know I don't take no well."

"I…"

"I called because I love you." The line went dead.

He knew the break-up was bullshit. She did love him. He would get her back, but first he had to deal with his enemy.

***

The Genoa infiltrator had the nerve to buy an estate only four houses down. It wasn't as big as Roman's but it was still huge. Valentina had sent over floor plans along with the name on the deed. It was under a corporation, but the signature was of someone he and the family had been in bed with for years. No more.

It was dark and he was dressed in all black. Instead of taking the sidewalk along the lake, he had kept to the shadows and had gone around the back. The house would have cameras, but he had taken a page from the enemy's book and had his hackers delay the footage at the right time so he wouldn't be seen stepping on the grounds. Luckily, the guy didn't have dogs either.

Dominic had done his part and his gift had been delivered earlier. Hopefully, Roman would be there at the right time to see him unwrap it. Gazing at his watch, it was time. He slid through the side fence right where his men had left an opening. He patted the gun under his coat once—a habit.

There would be few men on site tonight and the guys who'd be coming in the front would take care of them. A light came on in the large four-car garage. The gift had arrived and the guy in the garage was his to kill.

The camera feeds were paused to cover his entrance. He kept away from the lights and sneaked closer to the garage. Stopping briefly to let his eyes adjust to the bright light, he zeroed in on his target in front of a large wooden hull boat.

"Fenetti." Roman stalked toward the guy who'd betrayed his family. "Looks like you are really settling into the area. I didn't know we were neighbors and here you have a custom boat already." Roman seethed.

The man tried to appear calm, but his fingers were shaking. "Just keeping up with the Joneses, as they say, or in this case, the Caponellis. I heard you had a boat on order too. I might have to find a *local girl* to keep me warm at night, as well."

"My boat's not done yet."

"Yes, I wasn't expecting this so soon, but it came in." The guy walked around it, obviously trying to keep the vessel between them.

Roman rested a palm on the hull with the ease of someone who held the winning hand.

"What are you waiting for? Climb up and take a look," Roman urged.

Fenetti pulled at the lapels of his suit jacket and tucked at his shirt collar.

"Don't mind if I do." He snatched the nearby step ladder and set it by the boat. He steadied it with an air of resolve and took a few steps up. Fenetti's face went white, his breathing labored. Triumph pumped through Roman.

Fenetti stumbled down the ladder, fear on his face. The vein at his throat pulsated so vividly Roman could see it from where he stood.

"Something wrong?" Roman shoved aside the ladder offhandedly, never taking his eyes off his enemy. Fenetti was shaking from his shiny slicked back hair all the way to his ugly crocodile boots.

Dominic never failed to disappoint him. Roman knew what lay on the deck of the boat. The only thing left of the man who'd terrorized Madison—his tattooed hands. The severed limbs lay on the surface of the fresh wood, marring it with oozed blood that had probably dried to brown by now.

"Looks to me like you have *all hands on deck*," Roman joked. He voice rang with a sinister edge.

"What do you want, Caponelli?" Fenetti hissed like a stray cat backed into a corner.

"Why did you have to get greedy? We treated you well."

"I wanted more and I wasn't born into royalty like you were," Fenetti barked.

201

"You think I haven't done my share of the fuckin' dirty work?"

At that, Fenetti at least had the decency to turn away. Roman had worked his way up from the bottom. His father taught Roman how to be what he'd become. A complex businessman who wasn't afraid of doing whatever needed to be done. Evidence of that was lying on the deck of the boat beside him. His father made sure he knew what it was like to work the streets and move up by earning. The only difference was that Roman could now pay for the dirty work to be done. His empire had grown to the point where even this piddly shit didn't need to be done by him, but Roman never liked to take a backseat. So many empires had crumbled from the emperor hiding behind the castle walls.

"I didn't say that," Fenetti mumbled nervously. "But you're on my turf now." The guy rushed over to the door of the house. Roman followed calmly. Fenetti pushed a panic button.

"There's no use," Roman said on a bored sigh. "No one's going to save you."

Fenetti struggled with the doorknob, but it was locked. "My men will be here in a minute and you'll be dead. Then this whole town will be mine and so will the girl you've been banging." Roman's nostrils flared as Fenetti rambled on his bullshit. Scared, he retreated to the corner. His eyes searched for help that wasn't going to come. "Hell, maybe I'll bang her, then take her out myself."

Fenetti crossed the line by threatening Madison, his one true love. Roman's eyes turned murderous as he lunged. His large, strong hands wrapped around Fenetti's throat. The man wrestled, but Roman was too strong. He thrashed and sucked in a sharp gasp that fueled Roman's bloodlust. His feet kicked out and connected with a metal trash can.

This was it.

There was no going back.

Roman squeezed as Fenetti's knees gave out and he completely collapsed. Fenetti's face had turned bright purple, but Roman didn't care at all. This was Roman, the mobster. Fenetti had threatened his family, his empire, and his woman.

Roman dragged a slowly dying Fenetti into the cover of darkness, down to the dock, never loosening his hold around his neck. A tiny wave rolled in and the boat beside them clipped the side of the dock. Fenetti's thrashing slackened as unconsciousness claimed him, but Roman didn't let go until he felt his body become completely limp and the life left his eyes.

Dominic was there, waiting. Roman tossed his former friend's body down in front of him and walked away into the darkness of night.

Chapter Twenty-Three

"You look so handsome." His mother straightened her double strand of pearls as she stood beside him in front of the mirror. "You remind me of your father on our wedding day."

"You look beautiful as always, Mother," Roman replied as he tugged at his collar. It was a custom made tuxedo, but it felt like he was choking. The ivory vest would match the bride's gown and the peach corsage of the bridesmaids' dresses. Neither of which he'd seen or really cared about. His stomach protested with a pit of regret and hopelessness.

"What's wrong? You should be happy. It's your wedding day." His mother turned to face him.

"Yes, I should."

He wandered over to the window. They were at the Rinaldi mansion. The wedding would take place in the garden below. "I just can't believe that my father, of all people, would force me to marry someone I don't love." He turned around, feeling defeated and angry. "To spend my life in a loveless marriage," he mumbled with spite.

"*Shh*. Let's not talk about it anymore. Your father did what he had to do." She waved her hand. "We all do what we have to do for the good of the family."

"And I will do what I have to do to for the family, but it doesn't mean I have to like it." His voice was louder than he intended it to be.

His mother strolled over and sat in the chair nearest him. "I know, and in time, I hope you can forgive him for what he asked you to do."

There was a knock at the door and Arlo walked in.

"It's time." His enforcer was dressed also in a tux. He was like a brother and he needed the man he trusted most in the world beside him today. Roman knew that underneath his suit, the man was carrying at least two guns and a few knives. Would there be trouble today? Probably not, but one didn't get to be old in his line of work without being careful.

"I'll be right down." Roman took a deep breath. Never had he been so nervous before. Facing down a deadly enemy seemed insignificant compared to this.

"I brought you this." Arlo produced a glass from behind his back. "Just in case."

Roman eagerly took it and tossed the drink down in one gulp. His mother and Arlo both found it funny, but it just pissed him off more. He hadn't seen Madison in a week and it hurt like hell. It ached to think of her.

"Let's get this over with." He slammed the glass on a nearby table.

"Roman, you are supposed to enjoy your wedding." His mother now stood in front of him with her arms across her chest.

"Weddings are for women. The wedding nights are for men." He scoffed, wishing the whole fucking thing was over. His foul mood was getting the best of him. And then there were all the people he had to deal with afterwards. Make polite conversation with members of the Rinaldi family when all he wanted to do was punch them in the throat and seek out the woman he loved.

"Oh, Roman." His mother put her arms around him. "Try to enjoy the ceremony. Forget everything that has happened and start everything over today. You have a beautiful woman waiting down there for you. Don't leave her waiting too long."

"Don't worry. I will be on my best behavior." Or at least try to be.

"Good." She cupped his jaw in her palm and kissed his cheek. Arlo held his arm out for her and she accepted.

"We will see you downstairs."

He nodded and wandered back to the window. The guests were all in their cloth covered chairs waiting for the ceremony to begin. The Rinaldis had spared no expense. Bruno's daughter would have a wedding fit for a queen. If it had been up to him, his wedding would have been a private affair back in Genoa at Firenza and Madison would be by his side.

Swearing loudly, he shoved his arms in to his jacket and headed for the door.

***

Crossing Roman

Roman and his groomsmen stood at the front of
the aisle while all the guests faced them. It felt a
little like a lineup at the police station or a firing
squad to him. The priest weaved back and forth at
the center of the aisle. Perhaps Roman wasn't the
only one who'd had a drink before the show began.
The sun gleamed above and white fully clouds
floated by.

The ushers snapped out and rolled the white
cloth runner for the wedding party to enter on. A
couple of his cousins escorted the grandparents and
parents of both families down the aisle and to their
seats. His mother beamed as she walked down,
trailed by his father. Roman avoided eye contact
with the man, and seethed at seeing his face.
Rinaldi's new lady friend was escorted to her seat
up front by one of his lieutenants. Her elaborate hat
blocked the view of her face. He quickly turned his
gaze away, annoyed at the world.

Music floated in the air, signaling the ceremony
had started. A quartet played Pachelbel's Canon in
D. That was one of Madison's favorite songs. The
ache in his heart started anew and a forceful longing
welled within him. A pair of geese flew overhead.
They mated for life, but would he?

All eyes turned to the back as the wedding party
started to filter out from the house. A flower girl,
the daughter of one of Rinaldi's captains, was
greeted with smiles as she wandered down the white
runner dropping peach colored flower petals from
her basket. Behind her, the first of the bridesmaids
started down the aisle, each of them dressed in a
strapless peach color floor length gown and long

ivory gloves. He didn't know all of them and really didn't give a shit who they were. He focused on what they wore to keep his mind on something before he went crazy.

The last bridesmaid bore such a resemblance to Madison that his heart jumped in his chest. They could have been twins. He tugged at his collar again and exhaled deeply. Valentina, the maid of honor, came next. His sister was stunning. Her peach dress was a little different than the others. It was off the shoulder with an extra layer of fabric that trailed behind her.

At the sight of his sister, Roman smiled for the first time and his heart warmed. Yes, Valentina had been with him through thick and thin. She was always the dramatic one so it only made sense that her dress would be distinctive. Valentina linked arms with Arlo as they promenaded the last few steps. Roman stepped forward to kiss her on the cheek.

The quartet finished Pachelbel's song and started the wedding march. The tum, tum, ta, ta, tum reverberated in his ears, solidifying this as a done deal. This was it. There was no backing out now.

Everyone rose to their feet and held their phones and cameras close, hoping to get the first shot of the bride. Bruno Rinaldi came into view, his daughter's hand tucked in the elbow of his arm. He beamed with happiness. At least someone was happy. The bride's face was blurred by the extravagant veil she wore. Roman's chest tightened. His fist flexed. This whole mess wasn't her fault but he still felt anger and loss at the way things had played out.

Rinaldi and his daughter strolled slowly down the aisle. Guests strained to catch a glimpse of the bride. People *oohed* and *ahhed*. Nearing the end, Rinaldi stopped at his seat and gave the bride a hug. The man then accompanied his daughter closer and placed her trembling hand into his.

He whispered in Roman's ear. "Hurt my daughter and I'll kill you."

Roman scoffed.

Bruno lifted his daughter's veil and kissed her cheek. Her profile and rosy cheeks were familiar, and when the bride turned his way, Roman's heart soared in disbelief. The eyes that stared directly at him were Madison's, not Layla's. A rocket of different emotions pummeled him. Happiness, relief, confusion…and most importantly, love.

His bride stared up at him with unshed tears in her eyes. Roman must have had shock written all over his face as Madison whispered, "I'll explain later."

Right now, he didn't give a flying fuck what the reason was. All he cared about was that she was here beside him. He shook his head to clear the fog. Nothing mattered now except the woman beside him. He and Madison would be together forever.

The priest cleared his throat and they stepped in front of him. The ceremony was a blur as he only had eyes for his bride. She was a vision, a goddess. Her dark hair shimmered in the sunlight. Some of it was up in back with sexy ringlets framing her face. An image of what she might be wearing under the dress caused him to swallow and almost moan out loud. The dress she wore was one that she'd probably made herself. It was perfect and pure Madison.

He briefly admired the gown. The dress was obviously brand new but it could have been from a vintage couture collection. It was ivory lace covered with beads, crystals, and sequins. Not too many, but just enough to make it shimmer with her every movement. Instead of being strapless or off the shoulder like the others, hers was short sleeved with what he'd once heard her describe as a sweetheart neckline.

His mother insisted that he buy his bride a gift. The diamond necklace he'd sent to her room before the ceremony was now sparkling around her throat. Never had he dreamed that it would be for the one he truly loved. Had everyone known but him? He admired the rest of her gown. Her floor-length bridal dress hugged her curves and the small train was edged in more exquisite lace.

"Dearly beloved, we are gathered here today…." The Priest's voice became a dim sound. Roman was so elated and happy to be marrying the love of his life. Everyone stopped. Lost in his own thoughts, he realized the time had come.

He watched Madison hand her bouquet to Valentina to hold. Arlo nudged him and handed him a diamond wedding band.

"Roman, do you take Madison to be your lawfully wedded wife?"

"I do." He slipped the ring on her finger next to the large engagement ring he'd bought her.

"Do you, Madison, take Roman to be your lawfully wedded husband?"

"I do." The words coming out of her mouth made his heart jump. *I'm married to Madison.* All he knew was that she was now his.

"You may kiss the bride."

He leaned forward and stared into her eyes. They were luminescent and bright. It was different than any kiss they'd shared before. It was a kiss that promised devotion, honor, and love for all of eternity.

Chapter Twenty-Four

Roman

Roman did a double take at the woman next to his sister. The bridesmaid who resembled Madison was Layla. No wonder he didn't know it was her at first. He'd never seen her smile before. Now the girl had a grin on her face as wide as Valentina's. Stephanie was also part of the wedding party. The woman still hadn't warmed up to him, but hopefully she would get there soon.

The rest of the day passed in a blur and it couldn't be over soon enough. The receiving line had been full of handshakes, hugs, and best wishes. Their wedding cake was a mile high confection of peach and ivory flowers and the groom's cake was a chocolate one from the coffee shop where he first met his bride. Not that he ever had any doubts about marrying Madison, but the way it had come about was nonetheless stressful.

"Okay, Mrs. Caponelli." Roman loved the way that sounded when he referred to his new bride.

"Please tell me again how this miracle happened?"

"Believe it or not, it was my mother who saved the day." Her smile was breathtaking. "I guess many years ago, my mother and Bruno had a romance, but they'd parted ways." She paused to watch the two they spoke about waltz across the dance floor. "Months later, when my mother found out she was pregnant with me, she'd gone back to tell Bruno. Unfortunately, the woman Rinaldi would eventually marry had turned her away at the door, telling Connie that the two were already engaged. Worrying that if he found out, they might try to take the child, she kept my existence a secret until now."

If it weren't for Connie confessing that Rinaldi was in fact Mr. Smith, Madison's biological father, none of this would have taken place. His heart soared. Never in his life had he been so happy.

"It was a chance meeting years later, after Rinaldi's first wife had passed away, that the two rekindled their romance. My mother hadn't been traveling the world all this time, but secretly spending it with her long lost lover. Not only do I now have a father, but I've gained a sister as well. When I told her that you had to marry someone else, Mom left in a rush. I didn't find out everything until a few hours before. Why she waited so long to tell me the news was a wonder, but at least it ended happily. Maybe Bruno needed some convincing first? I really don't know and really don't care."

"I still can't believe it. Why didn't anyone tell me?"

"It happened so fast. Luckily, I had a dress to wear. Maybe they wanted to test your loyalty?"

"I doesn't matter and I don't care. All that's important is that I have you."

The two families were now united and the bride and groom were in love. It was a little faster than she wanted to get married but the end result was the same. He and Madison would be together forever. Roman had also, in some twisted way, kept his promise to his father.

Roman leaned against the wall and studied his guests. He admired his wife as she danced with her father. They had a lot of time to make up for.

The alpha part of Roman was mad at her father for being absent from her life, but there was no changing it.

"Everything is beautiful, Roman. Congratulations." An aunt Roman barely ever saw gushed at him. He kissed her cheek and she walked toward the ladies' room.

Arlo took a turn across the floor with Valentina, but he could have sworn the man had been watching his new sister-in-law, Layla, with more than casual interest. His eyes narrowed in bewilderment. Roman never really thought of Arlo with a woman. He was always so busy taking care of business it hadn't occurred to him that the man needed the warmth and love of a good woman by his side too.

Connie filtered through the crowd of guests, appearing right in front of him. "You got what you wanted. Don't *mess* it up." Her ominous tone was understandable, but nothing could ruin today.

"I won't," Roman acquiesced, and leaned down to kiss his new mother-in-law on the cheek. She walked away and Dominic stepped up.

He spied Stephanie slumped at a table giving him her usual evil eye. It was going to take some time to get her to warm up to him. When she turned her attention to the man standing next to him, her expression changed.

"Congratulations," Dominic yelled over the music.

"Thanks." He draped his arm over Dom's shoulder. "Let's step outside for a moment. It's getting stuffy in here." It wasn't, but he didn't need extra ears listening to their talk.

"You missed the ceremony." Roman handed him a cigar from his pocket. They clipped the ends of both their cigars, and he offered him a light.

Dominic inhaled the smoke and let it out slowly. "I had to take care of that business for you."

He knew the reason he was late. That's what he paid the guy for, to take care of business. Right now the body of Fenetti was probably at the bottom of Lake Michigan, never to be seen again, and if he knew Domonique's technique, the man was probably in numerous pieces as well.

"And how did that go?"

"You won't have to worry about that problem ever again." Dominic rewarded him with a rare smile. The man was loyal to a fault, but cared about nothing and no one. That made him both valuable and frightening at the same time. He was lucky Dom was on his side and *only* his side.

"Good man." He slapped him on the back. They stood smoking in silence. There was no more to be said.

After a few moments, Roman ushered him back

to the ballroom. "Find a nice girl to dance with and have some fun."

He just nodded and headed for the cake table. Roman observed Stephanie following him with her gaze. Arlo was now dancing with Layla. Rinaldi spun Connie around as Madison danced with his father again to a faster tune.

Taking a seat at an empty table, he took out his phone and grinned. Valentina had already posted some pictures from the wedding to her social media page. He looked at another post on her page and scratched his forehead. Why had his sister liked the page for the Genoa Police Department? Flipping to the page, there was a photo of Ryan Donovan with the force's new K-9 dog. Donovan smiled at the camera as he kneeled by their newest dog.

"What are you doing over here all by yourself?" Madison leaned down to kiss his head and slid into the chair next to him. She had been torn from his side a few times to dance, so it was a comfort to have her back where she belonged.

"Just looking at some of the pictures Val posted from today." His bride peeked over his shoulder.

"I don't remember seeing any dogs and cops here." She raised her eyebrows.

"I'm afraid for some reason, Valentina seems to have taken an interest in local law enforcement."

"Now don't get all in a knot, big brother. She's going to be a lawyer, so it's only natural that she'd want to keep up to date with what's going on in town."

He turned the phone off and slid it into his pocket. "Right now, the only thing that I'm interested in is you and seeing what you have on under this dress, my beautiful bride." He nipped her lips and caressed her cheek. "But first I have a gift for you."

"I don't need any more gifts. The only thing I want is you." She took his hand in both of hers. They had stopped shaking a long time ago and were warm to the touch. Her shiny diamond ring reflected the lights above.

"I think you'll like this one. Come with me." Roman rose and pulled out her chair. Together they weaved in and out between the dancers to get to the stage.

Grabbing the microphone from the DJ, they thanked everyone for coming, made their excuses, and escaped to his car. There was one location he needed to show her first before whisking her off to the honeymoon.

***

Madison

It was a two hour drive back to Genoa and Madison had drifted off to sleep with the quiet hum and rocking of the car. Wiping the slumber from her eyes, she stretched and glanced out the window. "What are we doing here?"

"I told you I had one more gift for you and this is it." Roman put the car in park.

She surveyed the damaged shell of the building that once housed the arts center and shook her head. "I don't understand." It wounded her heart to stare at the wreckage. It was such a tragedy. The place had been picturesque. "Why are we here?"

"When I first met you, you had a dream of becoming a designer and you gave that dream up for me." He spoke softly and entwined her fingers with his.

"I'll find a new dream," she said.

"I found one for you."

She tilted her head. "Don't worry. I'll find what I was meant to do in life."

"I'm not worried about that, but you love this town." He pointed with his other hand toward the rubble. "No one is a better person to represent the place and keep it the way it is. That's why I bought you this building. Or, should I say, the land it sat on."

Her eyes widened. "You did what?" She sat up straighter.

"You will oversee the construction and design of the new arts center, and the town's new department of tourism and historical society."

"Seriously?"

He smiled. "Yes, you can do whatever you want with it. It's your canvas."

"Oh, Roman." Madison threw her arms around his neck. "It's the best gift anyone has ever given me." Her lips touched his and she hugged him close.

"When can we get started?"

"Patience, my dear."

"But—"

"No buts." He shifted the car back into drive. "First I'm going to make love to my bride."

Madison kissed his cheek and briefly rested her head against his shoulder as he pushed the car into drive. Minutes ticked by and they sat in contented silence. Madison rested her head against the headrest and Roman's hand stayed firmly planted on her thigh. His occasional movement or rub made her hyper aware of him. The relationship had been fast, but she knew they were meant to be.

In the distance, an immense gray stone compound was sprawled against a hilly backdrop. They were winding up a long drive to the top. **'Castle of the Mountains Resort,'** the sign read. Roman pulled the car to the valet station.

"Welcome." A tall man layered in red addressed them. Roman tossed him his keys and came around Madison's side of the car. Another valet was there to open her door, but Roman practically shoved him aside. He reached down and took Madison's hand in his own.

"Shall we, Mrs. Caponelli?"

The smile that spread across his lips made her heart soar. Her feet had barely hit the pavement before he picked her up into his arms.

"I can walk." Madison laughed.

"Not today. You are going to be pampered and taken care of like the wife of Roman Caponelli should be," he informed her as he hurried straight past the check-in desk to the elevator.

"Where are we going?"

"You ask too many questions." He silenced her with a kiss.

The elevator doors slid open and Roman stepped in with Madison still cradled in his arms.

"Press the top button."

"The penthouse?" Madison raised her eyebrows. "Very impressive."

"Only the best for my bride," Roman replied. His lips never left hers until the door opened to their floor.

His long legs had them in front of their suite in no time.

"Reach into my pocket." Madison slipped her hand inside his jacket and found a rectangular key card. He lowered her enough to slip it into the door mechanism and Madison pushed down, swinging the door open.

A posh and opulent suite greeted them. Burgundy and gold accents were everywhere. It was fit for royalty, mafia royalty. The scent of flowers lingered in the air. Roman headed directly for a heavily carved set of double doors to the right. Inside, a huge bed complete with fluffy, thick pillows and a red down comforter lay before them. On a side table sat a vase of magnificent crimson roses and champagne chilled in a silver cooler.

He tossed her down on the soft bed and she bounced, giggling. Roman reached for the champagne and the pop of the cork sounded in the room. He filled two glasses and sat beside her.

"I don't think I have ever been this happy." He tapped his glass to hers. "To the beautiful, smart woman who agreed to be my wife." Madison's cheeks were rosy.

"I'm happy too," she said. "Ecstatic."

Roman finished his drink in one sip. Taking the glass from Madison, he set them both back on the side table.

In one fast move, he climbed on the bed and took her in his arms. Their lips met. Roman kissed her hard, like he couldn't get enough, and his new wife met him with just as much fervor. He slipped his hand inside her dress, cupping her breast, which was already pebbled with desire. His palm massaged it until he clasped only the tip and twisted gently. Madison's fingers explored the warm muscles of his back. Each wanted to mark the other as their own, a kiss here, a squeeze, a caress like none ever before. Roman's moans mingled with her own. Where one started, the other one would finish.

Madison stripped him of his coat and made short work of his shirt buttons, exposing his dark skin. Between passionate kisses, her hands roamed his hair-roughened chest. Roman hovered above her and his eyes were glazed with fire. He quickly removed her gown, leaving her bare except for her ivory thigh-highs. "I think I'll leave these on." The admiration in his gaze needed no explanation.

Madison lay with her eyes closed while his lips and hands roamed, caressing every inch of her flesh. His whisker roughened jaw added even more heat to her already flushed skin. He was fixated on her milky white breasts, the back of her knee, or some spot that needed attention and love. He stopped and reached behind him, taking a stemmed rose in his hand. Touching the delicate rose to her lips, Roman traced the soft petals along her neck, her collar bone, and across her breasts. She swallowed. The tenderness of the rose and the risk of a cut from a thorn kept her still. Her heartbeat pounded loudly in her ears, silent to the world. It was just the two of them.

No longer able to stay still, Madison took the rose in his hand and tossed it across the room. "Don't make me wait any longer to be yours."

"Patience, my love." He placed a finger on her lips and cradled her face in his hands. "You were mine the first time I laid eyes on you."

The man meant it. There was no doubt in her mind. Crossing Roman was not an option.

Roman shifted between her thighs. One hand stroked the lace edge of her stockings, the other now entwined in her hair. Locking eyes with her, he thrust inside and she was now his body and soul. The night burned with their love for one another. After all of the denial, danger, and obstacles, Madison and Roman were now one, bound together for life, for better or worse, and 'til death do they part—the way it was supposed to be all along.

Epilogue

"What do you mean, my money's no good?" Mr. Gilman pushed the personalized check in her direction, but Madison shoved it back his way. It was reminiscent of their exchange not long ago when he refused to host her fashion show. A lot had happened since then, a whole lot.

"I'm declining payment for your ad in the travel magazine." She folded her arms across her chest. Not only had she taken over the town's arts center, department of tourism, and the historical society, she'd also become the editor and chief of the new tourist guide for the area. Madison was extremely busy and loving every minute of it. Everyone was scampering to get choice advertising spots in the new magazine before the deadline and Mr. Gilman was no exception. Her wedding present from Roman was being rebuilt under her direction.

"But I need to be in the publication. Everyone will see the ad," he pleaded.

"I didn't say I wouldn't publish the ad, I just won't take payment for it." Madison pressed her lips together to keep from smiling.

"What? I don't understand." The guy was actually starting to sweat. Beads of perspiration dotted his forehead.

"Mr. Gilman, I got Roman to admit that he, shall we say, persuaded you to not rent your venue to me earlier this year." The man at least had the nerve to blush. "I don't blame you and in fact, if it weren't for you doing as he suggested, I wouldn't be married to the man right now." Madison crossed her legs and swung her foot. "So I figure I owe you."

His eyes widened. "Really?"

"Yes, so consider your ad free, and let me know if there is anything I, or the *family*, can do for you in the future."

"Ah, yes. Thank you."

"So, is an inside cover spot to your liking?"

Mr. Gilman's eyes just about bugged out of his head and he nodded vigorously. "Yes, that is very generous of you." He rose to his feet and stuffed the new useless check in his pocket. "Thank you very much." He nodded some more and she muffled to urge to giggle. "Have a good day, Madison, and we'll be in touch." Mr. Gilman shook her hand and said farewell.

Madison smiled to herself. What a wonderful feeling it was to love one's job. Sure, she liked designing dresses at one time, but her home town, its people, and its history was her real love—after Roman, of course.

She spied her husband coming up the sidewalk with Dominic by his side. The two were heavy in conversation. It was hard to believe that not too long ago she'd just about given up hope of ever finding a man to settle down with.

Granted being a part of a mafia family wasn't quite what she'd expected, but it was what she'd chosen. It was obviously written in the cards because her father was also in the mob. Madison had been so lonely for so long, and now she'd not only gained a husband but a sister and a father. Roman entered her office alone and drew her into a long, hot kiss.

She'd found her dream…and her *family* man.

Author's Note

I love to write stories that take place in my home state of Wisconsin. The inspiration for the setting of this story is the beautiful tourist town of Lake Geneva. I changed the name to Genoa for the story but forgot that there is a real town called Genoa in Wisconsin. Both are beautiful places to see so if you ever travel to Wisconsin make sure to visit both.

About the Author

Ginger Ring is an eclectic, Midwestern girl with a weakness for cheese, dark chocolate, and the Green Bay Packers. She loves reading, traveling, watching great movies, and has a quirky sense of humor. Publishing a book has been a lifelong dream of hers and she is excited to share her romantic stories with you. Her heroines are classy, sassy and in search of love and adventure. When Ginger isn't tracking down old gangster haunts or stopping at historical landmarks, you can find her on the backwaters of the Mississippi River fishing with her husband.

Facebook:
https://www.facebook.com/romancewritergingerring

Twitter:
https://twitter.com/GingerRings

Website:
http://gingerring.com/